EMMA TENNANT

The Autobiography of the Queen

A novel

Arcadia Books Ltd
15–16 Nassau Street
London W1W 7AB

www.arcadiabooks.co.uk

First published in the United Kingdom by Bliss Books, an imprint of Arcadia Books
2007
This B format edition published 2008

A catalogue record for this book is available from the British Library.

ISBN 978–1–906413–01-9

Designed and typeset in Minion by Discript Limited, London WC2N 4BN
Printed in Finland by WS Bookwell

Arcadia Books supports English PEN, the fellowship of writers who work together to
promote literature and its understanding. English PEN upholds writers' freedoms in
Britain and around the world, challenging political and cultural limits on free
expression. To find out more, visit www.englishpen.org, or contact
English PEN, 6–8 Amwell Street, London EC1R 1UQ.

Arcadia Books distributors are as follows:

in the UK and elsewhere in Europe:
Turnaround Publishers Services
Unit 3, Olympia Trading Estate
Coburg Road
London N22 6TZ

in the USA and Canada:
Independent Publishers Group
814 N. Franklin Street
Chicago, IL 60610

in Australia:
Tower Books
PO Box 213
Brookvale, NSW 2100

in New Zealand:
Addenda
Box 78224
Grey Lynn
Auckland

in South Africa:
Quartet Sales and Marketing
PO Box 1218
Northcliffe
Johannesburg 2115

Arcadia Books is the *Sunday Times* Small Publisher of the Year

The Castle

On a dull morning in September at her Scottish castle Balmoral, the Queen was packing an overnight bag.

She had never done this for herself before, and after negotiating the luggage storeroom (which she had never visited before) she felt too much attention would be drawn if she was seen dragging a heavy suitcase down the corridors to her private sitting room.

Besides, used as she was to every day of a tour being planned to the minutest sartorial detail, the Queen was certain her outfits would be waiting for her when she arrived at her destination. That she was not embarking on an official visit – that, in fact, no one knew where she was going, not even the Duke, her husband (he was asleep in his room), somehow did not contradict her lack of anxiety about a change of clothes once she was safely abroad. The Queen had never gone anywhere on her own; and the choice of handbag preoccupied her more than a fear of independence. Should she take (to accompany the small suitcase she had selected) the white bag or one that would match the pale lavender tweed she had chosen for the journey? The Queen had always been meticulously turned out and now she must achieve that level of perfection without a maid or a lady-in-waiting. The future, as she had clearly decided, must look after itself.

The fact was, the Queen had reached a time when it was preferable to look back and record the triumphs and quandaries of the past, than to gaze at an uncertain future. For over half a century, she had reigned as a model sovereign: dutiful, always ready to hear the complaints or demands of her people and to put these before her own wishes and interests. But now, one *annus horribilis* was set to follow another. The European Council of Ministers was about to declare that all EU member states must have a written constitution. Most had, the most notable exception being Britain, with its 'flexible' unwritten constitution. Rationalising this system into a form that might make sense to anyone else would whittle down the Queen's role, in her view a further step towards a republic; descendants such as Prince William might end up as no more than exiled royals in their own country.

And Balmoral, the monarch's most adored

possession, provider of peace since Victorian times for those beset with the troubles of governance and the stress occasioned by constant exposure to the public gaze – Balmoral was under threat and would in all probability no longer exist as a great private estate when the new Scottish laws on land owner-ship went through. The Queen would lose her rights to shoot and fish and go stalking deer over the glorious forty-thousand-acre estate. The miles of heather and grass and the quiet lochs would be trampled by ramblers and the sense of a haven from prying eyes would be quite gone. Add to that the most recent scandal, a kiss-and-tell story just extracted in the tabloids on Prince Harry by a prior girlfriend and the Queen's decision to leave the country she had served so loyally needed little explanation.

By the time the overnight bag had been filled with nightdresses and summer outfits (these all strictly long-sleeved) there were only ten minutes to go before the cab – she had seen the number scrawled in the pantry when inspecting the day's tally of pheasants – would be at the side turret door of the castle. There remained only the question of what to place in the handbag, and this problem caused the Queen some difficulty, as she had never looked in any one of the several thousand handbags given to her by ladies-in-waiting or the Mistress of the Bedchamber before going on a factory visit or a walkabout to meet her subjects. The Queen had never suffered a sniffle, which would have justified the existence of the Kleenex tissue lurking within the rigid confines of the handbag. Nor did she ever powder her face in public, which would have given meaning to the pristine compact and discreet lipstick to be found in an angular corner of the white shining leather handbag. So it was with a sense of breaking new ground – a taste of what was to come – that the painfully hard gold clasps were pushed apart and the interior examined.

When the Queen had noted that there was nothing in the white handbag, she walked to her desk where the pile of letters from her people was refreshed every day by new pleas for kindness, love or money – and she dug deep into the section where a secret drawer, fashioned for Edward VII a century before, contained her air ticket and a stash of jewels. The Queen selected the Cambridge emeralds (they had been the gift of Prince Francis of Teck, brother of Queen Mary, to his mistress and had remained in the drawer after the Prince's death from pneumonia caught while stalking at Balmoral) and popped them into her bag.

'Oh good,' the Queen said as she stepped out into the corridor and found to her delighted astonishment that the small suitcase sported a pair of wheels. 'Does one simply pull it down the stairs?' she asked – but for once, there was no one there to reply.

The Footman

'Good morning, Your Majesty.' The greeting, not one that would normally be encouraged by the Queen or other members of the royal family, came from a tall, heavy young man in footman's attire. As he stood and bowed, the Queen could be perceived to smile; that this type of encounter was also unexpected was borne out by the jumping into a landing cupboard of a scurrying housemaid, who had come up behind Brno (this was indeed the footman's name: he was from a part of Eastern Europe that no one could ever remember). 'All set, ma'am?' inquired Brno in a slightly louder voice than usual, this to conceal the sneezes of the maid trapped in goose-down pillows at his rear. 'Tickets, money, passport, ma'am?'

Brno had been solely responsible for making possible the Queen's escape from a world in which she no longer believed she had a part to play. Some weeks before, going at speed down the upper corridor with the aim of avoiding a royal duke banished to the high-up bachelor quarters after a particularly painful bout of publicity, Brno had dodged (as the maid had today) into a tall wardrobe and as he did so a clutch of British passports had flown his breeches and floated down a magnificent cedarwood spiral staircase to land almost exactly in front of the Queen as she went to take her corgis for a morning walk. The rest played out as if already planned: the Queen retrieved the passports, invited Brno back into her sitting room, and half an hour or so later, had the best forger in the country at her service. (The air ticket, too, had been procured as if by magic: a firm called The Westminster Travel Bureau had called in a Polish plumber to unblock their loos and Brno, on standby as he had been responsible for Slovenian sanitation in his youth, had made love to the charming young proprietor of the firm.) The Queen, seeing she had been booked to travel upper class on a Virgin Atlantic flight to the Caribbean, was reassured by the apparent assumption by Sir Richard Branson that she would prefer to go incognito in a class to which all her ladies-in-waiting, friends and more distant relatives belonged, rather than as royalty. Both the Queen and the Queen Mother, of course, were described by the aristocracy as irredeemably middle class; but Sir Richard had anyway not created that tariff.

'Yes, everything ready, Brno,' the Queen said.

'You'll send me a postcard, won't you ma'am?'

'A postcard?' For a moment the vision of a post-age stamp danced in front of the Queen – but she remembered the island of her destination had been granted independence some years back: God knows who or what they had put on their stamps. 'Of course I will,' the Queen promised Brno. 'And I know that not a word will be said to His Royal Highness about – about all this?'

'I leave the castle today,' Brno promised – and this was indeed true: as Sir Brno he had purchased a thousand acres in Transylvania on the proceeds from his passports and had booked Lord Rogers to renovate the mouldering castle there. By this evening, as the Queen's Atlantic flight headed west across the ocean, Brno would be entering Romania (newly elected to the European Union).

'I must say goodbye now,' said the Queen gently as she also realised their diverging paths and thanking providence that she need never have to think about Europe again. 'I wish you the greatest good fortune in your future projects.'

Brno was still bowing when the Queen, carried along by the excellent wheels on her suitcase (she had chosen to push it, like a pram), disappeared from sight round a bend in the corridor. 'Where the fuck's she going?' demanded the maid (her name was Louisa Stuart), as she climbed out of the cupboard and indulged in a lengthy coughing fit.

'She's not getting the fuck out, is she?' And as Brno shook his head and looked firm, the girl added that she'd most certainly do the same if she had the chance.

The Dogs

The Queen had walked past the dressing room where the Duke was installed (a euphemism: men who had long ago stopped sleeping with their wives found themselves in need of a dressing room, as these invariably contained a bed with a plump eiderdown and a washbasin in case the stay was protracted).

There had been no farewell, emotional or otherwise – the Duke would hear along with the rest of the nation that his wife had disappeared. To tell him now would be folly, for the Queen had generally obeyed her husband as the old wedding service said she should; and to find her plans thwarted would have been insupportable. She might be the sovereign, but the Duke was her spouse: even contemplating the tussle involved was out of the question.

One of the Queen's sons was upstairs in the

bachelor quarters, but she couldn't remember whether this was due to an abrupt return to bacherlordom due to divorce or some kind of a nightclub scandal splashed all over the papers. At any rate, she walked past the corkscrew staircase leading upwards and went down to the drawing room off the main hall. Here, in time-honoured tradition, her corgis awaited their morning greeting from the Queen, followed by walkies on the wide lawns of Balmoral. And, just as she expected, a chorus of excited yapping met her entry: Whisky, Sherry, Trifle and Drambuie leapt up at the trim, tweed-suited figure and an eager queue formed just below the Queen's left elbow. Here, normally, a carrier bag (the Queen liked to use the same one every morning until it wore out and had to be replaced) swung with its allotted ration of biscuits. One each – and the dogs had learned there would never be a second helping – and it was time for the fresh air and happy scampering over the grass.

But today, as the Queen noted with some consternation, she had not been handed a carrier bag and there was no sign of the dogs' pre-breakfast snack on any of the occasional tables in the drawing room. Trifle, who was the Queen's favourite, understood this first and set up a moaning sound not unlike the bagpipes with which the castle regaled important visitors on their first evening there. Sherry followed suit, a look of disbelieving disgust on her face (she was descended from the

Queen Mother's corgis and did not like to forego a treat). The Queen, subject now to an attack from the rushing dogs, fumbled with the clasp of her white handbag, and for a few seconds a tense silence ensued.

Dear, dear Brno! While saying his farewells, he had filled the bag with biscuits and the normal routine could be resumed. The Queen sighed with relief – really, Brno had thought of everything...

But she had to admit to a strange and utterly unfamiliar feeling when the biscuits had gone and the dogs crowded by the door to commence the morning walk which, for the first time since they had come into the care of the Queen, they would be refused before being abandoned. Like the rest of the realm, they would have to figure out their future for themselves.

The Queen couldn't say whether the feeling was fear, which she had never experienced, or sadness or excitement. She gazed down into the handbag and then snapped it shut rapidly when what appeared to be a row of green eyes glinted up at her. Of course, the Cambridge emeralds! Yet it was reassuring to see the travel folder tucked, with its air tickets and the maroon passport with her coat of arms on the cover, neatly inside.

The Queen didn't wear a watch, but at least fifty grandfather clocks in the castle boomed out the hour.

'Heavens!' murmured the Queen. 'It's later than I

thought...' and, tying a headscarf over her freshly-permed hair, she slipped from the French window out into the garden and then down the flight of stone steps leading to the east turret entrance to the castle. A baying and shrieking went up from the corgis in the drawing room. The Queen walked up to a battered-looking car parked by the turret door.

'Mrs Smith?' said the driver as the Queen pulled at the car door. 'Come round this way, love, and sit in front!'

It would be wrong to say that the departure of the reigning sovereign from her demesne was marked with a sense of history on this damp and cloudy day. No one saw the Queen – or rather, no one recognised her as she paid off the driver at Inverness station and carefully took her reserved seat on the express train to London King's Cross. Later, when the paparazzi were swarming around Balmoral – and the other royal residences as well (it was said that the Duke (a) had run off with a floozy (b) decided to drown himself off Holkham Beach near Sandringham (c) was holed up at Windsor Castle where mobile phones were famously lacking in a signal) – many people would claim to have stood behind the Queen at airport and railway stations all over the country.

But no one could give any details of the Queen's destination or of the name she had travelled under.

On the day the Queen left her realm, only the corgis knew that something momentous had happened. And Brno, of course, but, being of a more extravagant nature than the monarch of the country that had given him the right to call himself her loyal subject, Brno was in his private jet to Transylvania before the train bearing the royal personage had even got to Crewe.

Escape

'Did anyone give you anything to put in your suit-case?' The check-in girl at Gatwick Airport sus-pected the small woman with white hair who stood in front of the desk might be deaf. She had asked the question once already, and (she glanced down at the prepared ticket and boarding pass) Mrs Gloria Smith had not answered. True, it seemed unlikely that a lady of advanced years carrying an unused-looking white handbag would be approached or persuaded to pack explosives by a terrorist – but you never knew, a respectable granny could outdo the Shoe Bomber any time.

The Queen was silent because she had never been on the receiving end of such a question before. How could anyone have given her anything to put in her suitcase when she had packed it herself for the first time in her life? At any other time, any one of the royal packers might have been asked to carry contraband by a bent footman or a naughty housemaid trying to send a gift in the protected – like a diplomatic bag – luggage which accompanied the Queen and the Duke on their tours. But today? The Queen decided it was best to tell the truth. 'Certainly not. One packed oneself, as it so happens.'

Check-in paused – she had been about to press down on her mobile and ask a colleague to come over when Mrs Gloria Smith failed to reply; now, the reply was more baffling than the previous silence. If this was a mentally ill passenger, why had there been no forewarning from the travel agent? Why had no one even booked a wheelchair?

'Did you ask for assistance, madam?' asked Check-in. She pressed the button on her mobile and a young security guard with a foxy expression made his way up to the desk. Luckily, this was the Upper Class check-in and most Upper Class passengers had already been provided with their hospitality vouchers for the Executive Lounge. Only two people stood impatiently behind this difficult and slightly suspicious traveller: they were a couple in their fifties or sixties who were now fidgeting and sighing with impatience.

'Certainly not!' the Queen repeated. It was true, she had looked rather longingly at the buggies carrying disabled travellers (though most looked perfectly fit) as Check-in had informed her right at the beginning of the procedure that Gate 37 was 'a mile and a half's walk'. But memories of Princess Margaret in her wheelchair at that disastrous photo shoot on the lawn of Clarence House stiffened the Queen's resolve to walk – after all, Glen Bogle was at least five miles in length and she walked along it regularly, with the Duke carrying a gun for a bit of rough shooting. Now, from the whispered tones and worried glances directed at her from Security and Check-in, she might as well be carrying a gun herself, the Queen thought: this was all a tremendous waste of time; and a royal tour, planned to the last half-minute, would have been airborne in the time this nonsense had taken. (Of course, the Queen remembered being asked to approve a battalion of armoured vehicles to be stationed at Heathrow in March 2003 by Tony Blair, the assault on Iraq having just begun. Care had to be taken. But the operation had looked unnecessary on TV, when the Queen watched over tea at Sandringham, and she had wondered at the time and many times since what good the invasion had done to anyone.)

'Thank you, madam. Here is your voucher for the Executive Lounge,' Check-in said when Security had given an invisible nod which cleared Gloria Smith of any supposed evil intentions. 'Thank you, sir,' now came in a warmer voice as Check-in noted that her new customers were titled; they were Sir Martyn and Lady Bostock and not in a good temper after being made to queue behind a little old lady who didn't look as if she'd ever been on a plane in her life.

'At last,' said Lady Bostock meaningfully as they all stood for a second staring at the back view of the small figure as it made its way down towards Departures.

'I'm so sorry to have kept you waiting, Lady Bostock,' Check-in purred. 'Now there aren't any pods left together, if you don't mind...'

'I do mind,' snorted Lady Bostock. She knew, somehow, that this inefficient person had given away the pods they wanted. (She knew also, from frequent trips, that these were curved chromium nests for one person: to communicate with a spouse or loved one meant adjacent pods, and these could not now be provided.)

'I'll see what we can do,' Check-in promised. There had been something that had flustered her about the old lady and she had let down the kind of passengers that Upper Class had been created for. Glancing up again, she saw the lady in the lavender tweed vanish in a queue by the gates to Departures and she tried to rid herself of her unease by stamping the electronic air tickets of the equally flustered Bostocks.

This sense of confusion and uncertainty may have accounted for the fact that the Queen's suitcase, which had been pushed to one side of the conveyor belt while she was questioned, remained there and failed to be included in the luggage on board the Virgin Atlantic flight to Hewanorra Airport, St Lucia. Eventually, when Check-in had completed her shift, the overnight bag was found and taken to be blown up by the authorities.

'Poor old thing,' murmured Sir Martyn (he was kinder than his wife), when the old lady disappeared from sight and it was time for the Bostocks to make the best of the short time remaining to them in the Executive Lounge. But Lady Bostock had seen the wheels peeping coyly from the base of the bag, and she now spoke loudly so all those responsible for passengers in Upper Class could hear her.

'I can't *think* what kind of people go out to the island these days,' Lady Bostock said. 'It really has changed, darling, hasn't it?'

The Pod

The Queen, due to her height, was invisible in the pod she had been politely but firmly moved to after pressure from the unpleasant-looking late middle-aged couple who had now been reunited in adjacent accommodation. A glance at the label on their cabin baggage rewarded her with the information that they were Sir Martyn and Lady Bostock; and a distant memory returned, of knighting Bostock and of his Lady gushing at the reception after the ceremony. The Queen, not for the first time, wished the whole process of conferring honours and titles could be reversed, and instead of 'Arise, Sir Martyn' there could be the opposite, where the wretched recipient of a baronetcy, an OBE or a life peerage could sink instead to both knees and crawl away out of the door. The royal smile, obviously, never betrayed this hope.

Today, the Queen had to admit to herself, she

had been awarded black looks and rude stares from the intolerable Lady Bostock – and the fact that an unsmiling face was a feature never before witnessed by the sovereign (except on occasions of discussing imminent divorces and dodgy remarriages with her children) occurred to her forcibly as she pulled brochures and a grandly inscribed menu from the pocket in the leather side (this, like the seat, moved to provide a bed when required) of the pod. As she pondered the unusual sight of a frown (Sir Martyn) and a succession of withering glares (his wife), the Queen noticed in herself a feeling of acute discomfort, also previously not experienced on any public occasion. It must be indigestion, she decided; and although the Queen of England was known never to have suffered a day's illness in her life – or to have visited a sick relative in hospital, for that matter – it was known to the staff of Balmoral, Sandringham, Buckingham Palace and Windsor Castle that the monarch was partial to Bisodol when certain festive occasions had provided the rich food she disliked. Now, she wished she had packed the famous remedy, in the yellow and blue tin which had remained the same since her childhood. Perhaps – if she rang and asked the stewardess – but only a leaf-shaped diamond-bright light came on when she pressed what she took to be the bell. At the same time the seat shot forward and the Queen was almost propelled into the wide central aisle of the Upper Class section of the plane. Across the aisle, a man tapping frantically into his laptop gazed for a second at the old lady. Then a stewardess came up and asked if a choice for dinner had yet been made. 'Bisque d'homard in a neige of calabash,' the stewardess announced in a threatening tone.

The Queen liked to think she could deal with awkward situations (people when in her presence were frequently ill at ease and needed a simple topic to take their minds off the terrifying fact of meeting royalty) and, seeing that Lady Bostock was now staring from over the pod wall which separated them, she searched her mind for the easiest and most acceptable of these. Did you have far to come? was obviously out of the question, when you were seated at 35,000 feet and travelling at five hundred miles an hour; and it would look nosy to inquire whereabouts in London the Bostocks lived. Even the Queen's trained memory could not provide a postal code for them; but she had an inkling it was Belgravia.

Help came in the shape of the glossy brochure the Queen had pulled from the pouch a short while before. Here – and replicated she knew in a smaller form in the folder that Brno's friend at the Westminster Travel had prepared for her and which now lay at her feet in the white leather handbag – was the destination the Queen had chosen for her retirement from the stresses and strains of life as the Nation's Head. It was possible, indeed,

probable, that the Bostocks were also headed for
the acres of lush rainforest sloping down to the sea
on the Joli Estate – she hoped not but at least they
would have something in common if this turned
out to be the case. But 'Do you plan to stay long?'
somehow came out all mangled, in the face of Lady
Bostock's contempt and Sir Martyn's embarrass-
ment. It reminded her of the time, in a cramped
East End flat, on a tour of the then new high-rise
block, when the Duke had spotted a suitcase on top
of the bedroom cupboard and had asked if a holiday was planned. The answer, once the bafflement
of the tenants was safely avoided, with 'Do you
have far to go to work?' turned out to be simple:
there was nowhere else in the flat for storage. But
with the Bostocks – and the Queen had a feeling
now that their house in Chester Square had been
the venue for a reception (the Countess of Wessex
had probably attended it) for a visiting Saudi bil-
lionaire – it was going to be quite different. The
Bostocks were rich and upper class and clearly felt
no need to disclose their address while on the
island.

'One is so looking forward to seeing one's house
at Joli Estate,' the Queen ended rather lamely.

But she had seen – and she refused the lobster
and the medallions of lamb and nibbled at the
cheese and biscuits in order to calm her stomach –
that when Lady Bostock opened her vanity case and
pulled out a brochure, it displayed a picture of a

large hotel, with 'Joli Hilton' written in gold lettering across the page. Lady Bostock settled down (in a most familiar way, the Queen thought: she had never been subjected to public displays of affection and had had to ask a grand-daughter the meaning of 'snogging' a while back) and nibbled Sir Martyn's ear in a manner considered by the Queen to be very vulgar.

The Queen saw this display because she had risen to her feet prior to visiting the Upper Class lavatory, and had inadvertently looked over the rim of her pod.

What struck the monarch later as she emerged from the WC and made her way, eyes down, to her newly made-up bed, was the fact that she had risen to her feet and the Bostocks, not to mention the other passengers, had remained firmly seated.

The Other Side of the World

'Where to, ma'am?' The driver of the battered bus in which the Queen found herself was a big, burly black man in shorts and a green vest which had seen better days. His radio was on and from here, the first disappointment for the Queen, a stream of incomprehensible sentences emanated. Some words were in French. She had hoped, after recent banquets at Buckingham Palace with the impossibly arrogant French President of the European Union seated next to her, not to hear the language again once she was safely ensconced on territory she knew to be a part of her beloved Commonwealth. The words, most of them, sadly, impossible to understand at all, were clearly some kind of debased tongue, a patois that was most unacceptable to the Queen. That 'Where to, ma'am?' summed up his repertoire in English – and this in an American accent – quickly became apparent and this caused some anxiety for the Queen, especially as the muddled-sounding slang was in use when speaking into his mobile, while at the same time he used his knees for both steering the van and changing gear. But there had been hitches on previous royal tours and recalcitrant or dangerous drivers had been weeded out and replaced with an equerry – sometimes even the Duke himself. There was nothing to worry about – this, the Queen reminded herself, was an adage of the late Queen Mother and had proved on every occasion to be right, since even wartime visits to bomb sites had produced, with the help of a dry martini, a supremely unworried expression on the face of the King's consort.

'Number Five, Bananaquit Drive,' the Queen instructed the man who was to ferry her to a new life amongst her erstwhile (but surely still grateful) subjects. Independence had been granted in 1979. There must be many who wished they were still under the protection of their Queen.

The driver glanced over his shoulder at his elderly female fare with some surprise. His card said Alvyne Smith. It dangled along with a plastic Christmas tree above the steering wheel, so the Queen for a moment wished that Brno had come up with a more inventive surname for a departing monarch than the ubiquitous Smith.

'Où ça?' bellowed Alvyne as a jumbo shrieked overhead, the very plane, as the Queen saw, which had brought her here a couple of hours before. A pang (the Queen had never felt homesick, even on trips to safaris, African kingdoms, Australian garden parties and the rest, so she was at first, as with the open hostility of the Bostocks, able only to envisage indigestion as the enemy within) brought her sharply to the side window of the van: one always rid oneself of these tiresome complaints by concentrating on one's subjects. Who she would meet – and vitally, indeed more frequently now the globe had shrunk over the years to accommodate the royal tours and their inevitable repetition – the names and details of those she had met on earlier occasions were provided by a lady-in-waiting on a printed sheet. It would be bad form to ask of a person whether they had come far to meet their reigning sovereign if they'd given the answer before. Of course, people moved house all the time these days, so that particular ploy was fairly foolproof, but the occasion when Lady Emily had been down with flu and the startled pensioner had had to remind the Queen that she and her family had famously come over from Ireland just before the last walkabout and Her Majesty must surely remember this, had made the Queen wary. And today, of course, there was no lady-in-waiting, and there never would be again.

The delay in the emergence of the Head of the British Nation on to the tarmac outside Hewanorra Airport had been due to a combination of circumstances, most of these in one way or another connected to the Queen.

First, there had been the oddity of the US hundred-dollar notes distributed by an old lady to some of the roughest-looking porters, men from Vieux Fort with a history of crime – and the equally astonishing fact that not one of these men appeared prepared to accept the bounty so generously offered. Pouncing on the neat, lavender-tweed-suited figure as she emerged from Customs (where she had been arrested for failing to fill in a form: this was eventually supplied by a customs broker who wrote down the name and address of a Mrs Gloria Smith, Joli Estate) a gaggle of porters had demanded of the Queen that she indicate her luggage so they could wheel it out into the arrival bay and call her a cab.

But the Queen, who had now taught herself to ask the cost of things, demanded to know how much this service would be – and it was this which caused an uproar, as different currencies such as EC (Caribbean dollars) and even sterling and francs (Martinique, only twenty miles across the sea, was regularly visited by those who could afford the trip) were shouted out in the baggage hall. The Queen, flustered by the chaos caused by her simple question, had pulled her travel folder from the white handbag; and seeing ONE printed next to an unfamiliar (presumably American) face, she had removed a bill and then another, until a gust of wind from the open doors on to the concourse removed and distributed the rest. The honesty of the customs broker (the Queen, forgetting she had, at least nominally, abdicated, promised silently to award the man at least a CBE in the New Year honours) and the swift realisation that these were hundred-dollar notes, brought a moment of indecision to the swarming porters. Finally, threatened by the customs broker, they handed over the money, although at least half was missing when the Queen arrived at her final destination and with the dogged sense of order which had characterised her reign as sovereign, counted out the greenbacks and compared the sum to the neatly-written note accompanying the documents.

But where the Queen would spend the remainder of her years now occupied her thoughts more than any other. So far, the landscape of the southern part of St Lucia was similar to the brochure: lush, with flamboyant trees and coconut palms and banana plants poking up in dense undergrowth. There were few houses, but those that stood by the road appeared generally well maintained. They were made of wood and they had red roofs and sometimes people sitting on a veranda or out the back, under the shady tree in the garden. At a small, dusty place above the village of Choiseul, Alvyne stopped the van and went into a barn-like building, emerging with a crate of bottles marked Piton Lager; and here the Queen was able to glance past him as he emerged, and saw a dusty billiards table and a gaggle of youths. The Queen approved of youth hostels, and of efforts made to keep occupied those who would otherwise be liable to turn to crime – and for a moment, as Alvyne tried to force the ancient van back to life, the young of the hamlet above Choiseul saw an old lady with white hair smiling at them from the back seat. Then the door of the hall was kicked shut and the van shuddered, roared and moved on. But by this time, the Queen of England and Head of the Commonwealth – the woman to whose recent Jubilee the people of Britain and her past dependencies had flocked with love and joy – had turned to look from the window at the sheer impossibility of the Gros and Petit Pitons, rising, as they did, two thousand feet out of the sea.

'Heavens!' the Queen said.

'Pitons!' Alvyne said. He could glimpse his passenger's excitement at the sight of these giant needles, volcanic fossils clad with green tropical vegetation. (He had also noted the hundred-dollar bills so freely dispensed by his passenger at the airport and had agreed with himself that doubling the usual tariff of fifty bucks was only fair, given the problems that lay ahead when they arrived.)

'Are we nearly there?' asked the Queen. Alvyne thought he had seldom seen anyone so excited – not of that age, at least

'Non Bananaquit,' Alvyne replied, for he had not fully understood the query. Also, it did seem kinder to warn the Queen what she was likely to find. 'Non Joli,' Alvyne repeated several times.

But, 'Je pense qu'ils sont très jolis,' said the Queen. If the people here could only communicate in French, then she must address them in that language. 'Numéro cinq, Bananaquit Drive,' she added with the piercing clarity familiar to those at home who still listened to the Queen's Christmas broadcast. 'Combien de kilomètres encore?'

Alvyne ignored this question and made a play of concentrating ferociously on the road – which dipped down, lost its new-tarmac appearance and entered a series of ill-constructed hairpin bends. He reached for a beer from the crate on the front passenger seat and placed it between his knees. Looking into the rear-view mirror, he noted a serene expression on the face of the elderly lady, and attacked the beer-top with his teeth. The van swerved, and the Queen, hanging from a strap, narrowly missed being thrown first on to the floor and then out through the open van door and on to the road.

'Où sommes nous maintenant?' the old lady demanded, as the road now ran through open country and a small town could be seen in front of a blue stripe that was the sea.

'Soufrière,' Alvyne yelled, as he accelerated down the hill past a group of backpackers gathered round a large noticeboard, announcing the entrance to the Botanical Gardens. Large letters gave this as the birthplace of a royal personage, l'Impératrice Joséphine.

But to this piece of information the Queen did not respond. Slightly worried – had the old lady suffered a stroke, had he offended her in some way? – Alvyne could not have known that the second of these possibilities was in fact the correct one.

'One didn't come all this way,' said the Queen grimly in an undertone (and in English: she had no wish to offend the driver, after all), 'one simply didn't expect to have to take in Napoleon!'

Dream Home

From Soufrière – where, as was reported on the local radio in the ever-present patois of the island, a van had been implicated in a brawl in the main street and two eighteen-year-old men arrested – the road climbed steeply once more, this time through green lawns bearing shop-window arrangements of bougainvillea and hibiscus and coconut palms waving in a faint breeze from the sea. Joli Estate, said a large notice, as the van, spluttering at the effort in first gear, heaved its way above the Joli Hilton Hotel, the main reception and the high-up cottages, each with its plunge pool, allotted to the second rank of visitors. Seventy-five lots, Joli Estate, more boards insisted, as the road curved higher and the Pitons, like dinosaurs frozen on their deep base in the waters of the Caribbean, pushed in and then disappeared again from view as the Queen stared from the window and hung on to the strap.

One had been held up, of course, by the activity – so the Queen had chosen to label the brawl in the run-down and pitted streets of Soufrière. A gun had gone off, and it was perhaps this that had jolted her into realising she was not witness – as she and the Duke had been countless times in all the far-flung previous colonies they had visited and revisited in fifty years of the Queen's place on the throne of Great Britain – to a ritual dance or ceremony. This had been the real thing. Nevertheless, there had been something theatrical about it all; and yawns had to be concealed, as they had so regularly been in past days.

Alvyne jammed on the brakes at the point, high above the valley, where the words Bananaquit Drive were prominently displayed on a white board. The paint on the board was peeling; and the Queen, met invariably on official visits by coats of fresh emulsion or shining white gloss, assumed that the new distressed look, of which her younger relatives had informed her, was the intention of the decorators responsible for the development of Joli Estate.

That none of the lots had a house – or pool or anything else, for that matter – became clear once the Queen, refusing a helping hand from the driver (royals, especially the monarch, cannot be touched; a hand in the back or, worse, a familiar nudge is disallowed on all occasions), had descended from the van and looked around her. Banana plants were plentiful up here, certainly – but of Bananaquit

Drive, or any other signs of development, there were none. Here and there it appeared that an effort had been made, before the project had been abandoned; and it was by a hole in the ground at what could have been designated as No. 5 that the Queen stood for a while, until the heat drove her back to the van.

Alvyne was sorry for the old lady. He had tried to tell her what she would find here, but she hadn't understood.

It was downhill all the way to the stopping-place of the shuttle bus which would convey the Queen to the reception of the Joli Hilton, and Alvyne, aware that his fare had a wallet stuffed with American dollars, felt proud of himself later for taking only the routine fifty before driving off. There had been something about the small, upright figure with white hair and a large, old-fashioned-looking handbag, which had reminded him of his childhood – though he would not consider that this might have been inspired by a memory of pictures of the sovereign at the time of St Lucian independence. All the way back to Vieux Fort, the driver of the battered van puzzled over what would happen to his recent fare. There was something odd and unworldly about her – what if the hotel was full up and she had nowhere to go?

But she had money, of course, and he was glad he hadn't ripped her off. She'd be fine.

Reception

Reception at the Joli Hilton had found it difficult to place the Queen when the shuttle bus from higher up the Joli Estate valley brought her – and a handful of American tourists in identical T-shirts and shorts – down to the main desk in the building. The old lady had no luggage and had appeared surprised when they pointed this out – though where she thought her suitcase could be it would be impossible to say – but she carried an expensive, if out-of-date handbag, and soon opened this to reveal a travel folder containing a reassuring amount of US dollars. Jolene, the girl whose task it was to settle guests into their accommodation, reported later that, on catching a glimpse of the interior of the bag, she had thought she had seen something shiny; but women often tucked jewellery into their handbags, so nothing more was thought of it.

On the other hand, why did Mrs Gloria Smith not ask if she might lodge her valuables in the hotel safe? A campaign to spread the information that the hotel – indeed the entire island – suffered no crime, had been started a few weeks back, but no one had believed in it so it had been dropped as a waste of money. Could the old lady have understood herself and her possessions to be safe here? It seemed unlikely, as the lavender tweed suit proclaimed a very recent arrival. Reception decided to lodge Mrs Smith in the block of rooms just above the main desk: she didn't look like someone who would demand a plunge pool, and they could keep an eye on her more easily than if she were placed in one of the cottages higher up.

'If there is no sign of one's luggage, then one must buy some new clothes,' said the Queen. She was staring past reception at the boutique where various floral silks and enticing bikinis were laid out. Unsure whether she should ask opening hours (being the Queen had meant she had never seen a closed shop or an empty mall) the Queen paused before exposing herself in this way.

'Of course, madam.' Jolene, who now had developed a healthy curiosity on the subject of the old lady – perhaps she was looking for a companion, some visitors to the island actually came looking for such a person – moved a little closer to the Queen. Marriages, these normally performed on the beach by Father Kit Maloney (expelled from St

56

Winifreda's in Fitzrovia some years ago for molest-
ing choirboys and now ensconced permanently in
the village on Joli Beach) were fairly frequent –
same-sex nuptials proving the latest fad, but Jolene
did not consider a wedding for herself and Mrs
Smith. As she guided the frail but determined-look-
ing new resident of the Joli Hotel to the glass door
of the boutique, however, an idea came to her and
she slid off sideways, mobile phone appearing suddenly from under her hair.

'Excuse me, madam.' The concierge, as the
printed notice on the desk proclaimed him, jabbed
the form he had been filling in with the help of the
Queen's passport.

'What is it?' Being addressed first was simply not
on: everyone knew that people had to wait for royalty to make a remark, pose a question (or, very
unusually, make a joke) and his careless attitude
was exasperating. Of course, the Queen had to
remind herself that she was now Gloria Smith, but
this was tiring: she had had a long day and wanted
only to be shown her room, take off her shoes and
lie on the bed.

'Your address in the UK, Mrs Smith,' pressed the
concierge. 'We need to fill in here, madam –' And,
as irritated by the old lady as she was with him, he
pushed the form along the desk.

'The Foreign Office, London,' the Queen snapped. And, used as she was to being obeyed, there
was no sign in the Queen's demeanour of surprise

at the acquiescence of the concierge to her command. People had always done what the Queen wanted – that was why she loved the dogs so much, because they so often refused to do as they were told – and now, thinking of them and of the row of towels laid on the lawn every morning at Balmoral, and the green wellies set out there for herself on the long walks down glen and up brae, her eyes felt an unaccustomed moistness.

'This way, Gloria!' Jolene had decided on an informal approach since speaking on her mobile: she was quite new here and had called a friend to ask how she should handle the old lady. Staff at Joli were trained to chat and sit with visitors after carrying their rum punches across the beach from the Rainforest Bar – should she ask Mrs Smith now whether she would like a cocktail in her room or offer her a reflexology session (she looked as if her feet were causing her pain).

The Queen, who had never been called Gloria, did not reply, but walked straight up to the glass door of the boutique.

'I'll go for the manager,' Jolene said when the door failed to open. Nothing was going as it should, and her idea of gaining a holiday in England in return for a friendship in St Lucia now seemed a foolish one. Mrs Smith was the type who knew what she wanted and although it was clear that she was used to some kind of personal assistance – she had handed her bag over to Jolene before making

her unsuccessful attempt to gain access to the boutique and taken it back immediately after seeing the
door was locked – she didn't look like someone
who wanted a friendly chat, or even a friend, for
that matter. There was something odd about the
old lady, Jolene thought – but perhaps the English
were all like that. Coming from a village high above
the Joli Estate, Jolene had taught herself English
from watching the new satellite TV installed there
recently, and her chief picture of those who resided
in the UK was inspired by *EastEnders*. The wedding
of Charles and Camilla had also been popular on
the island – but it was hard to know which pro-
gramme gave the most truthful picture of that far-
away country as both worlds seemed simultaneously
real and unbelievable.

By the time Jolene had been called to the desk by
the concierge and told that her friend Austin was
outside waiting for her, the Queen had pressed the
Up button by the lift and was about to enter when
Jolene called out to her to go to Room 209 on the
second floor. At which – and the transformation
came as a complete surprise to staff personnel – a
smile lit up the old lady's face in the most extraordinary way. All at once, as concierge and Jolene
conveyed to each other with their mutual looks of
astonishment and pleasure, the old lady became
someone whose approval and happy attentions
were highly desirable and impossible to forget once
experienced.

So it was that the Queen, still wearing her radiant smile, rose to the second floor of the Joli Hilton, smiled again at the cleaning woman who emerged from Room 209, mop in hand (this was fortunate, for the Queen had neither key nor card to gain entry) and was able, at last, to take a brief nap on the bed.

A House Without a Head

By the time the Queen had fallen into a blissful sleep peopled by figures from her now-abandoned past – her children were not amongst these, but her grandson William, as so often before in her dreams, appeared in his Coronation robes and stooped low to kiss his sovereign – the sun was beginning to climb down the sky in St Lucia and, at Balmoral, the gloaming, the lovely, late purplish evenings to be found only in Scotland, was turning with the presence of a new moon in the sky, to night.

Louisa Stuart, the maid, had been the first to set up the alarm – although, as members of the staff were shamefaced to admit, it wasn't until nearly midday that the Queen's absence was noted; and, due to a peculiarly irritating bureaucracy, it was one p.m., the usual time for luncheon to be served at the castle, before the Duke was told of his wife's disappearance. In corners of tartan-clad turrets courtiers and servants conferred: phones were picked up in the library and on the advice of the Chamberlain put down again for fear of bugging. The corgis, found in the seldom-visited third drawing room, were chased from the room they had angrily savaged and fouled once the permanence of their mistress's absence became probable. Dew fell on the towels laid out for the dogs on the east lawn; and the Queen's wellies set out there stood unfilled and glistening in the first shower of the September day.

'She had a wee case,' Louisa, pink with triumph, was recounting her experiences in the butler's pantry. Mrs McDuff, the housekeeper, and a gaggle of maids pressed their bodies against the plate cupboard to hear her and over by the sink a glass smashed, apparently of its own accord – which added to the atmosphere of hysteria. 'A wee case on wheels, ye ken. She was pushin' it along when he –'

'I always knew that Brno was no good,' Mrs McDuff said. 'You must have eyes in the back of your head, Louisa,' she added in a reproving tone. 'Her Majesty would never use a wheeled suitcase. And you don't push them, you pull them. Don't give us a whole lot of fairy stories, now.'

But the maid was adamant. She remembered the Queen pushing the case along like a pram – or a child's buggy – and she distinctly had the impression that Her Majesty was leaving for good.

'But why would she do that?' cried Mrs McDuff. She was an ardent royalist and it seemed impossible that the monarch, after all these years of service to her people, could envisage walking out on them. Surely, she was simply taking a short break – although this was most unlikely too, especially with of all things a wheeled suitcase.

'She was goin' somewhere hot,' Louisa gloated – for she had seen the sticker saying PalmVil Holidays that had fluttered from the shiny white handbag before Brno caught it and crumpled it up, then consigned it to a trouser pocket. 'Lucky old Queen,' Louisa said irreverently.

A gong sounded from the main hall of the castle. Mrs McDuff shook herself and the plump maids shivered as a door opened and the head butler looked in at the crammed pantry. He demanded to be told whether they were aware that luncheon was about to be served. Could they get the hell out of his pantry, please? Where was Tom the footman? What the blankety-blank was going on today?

'Mr Struthers, we have some important news for you,' Mrs McDuff said in a portentous tone.

But before she could speak, the electrically-operated lift (installed at Balmoral in the early years of the twentieth century) groaned up from the kitchens, bearing a platter of eggs in aspic, each decorated with a scoop of mayonnaise and a mini-ature tomato. Struthers pulled the lift door higher, the maids, gasping and giggling, left by the side door leading down to staff quarters and Tom the footman finally appeared just as the kilted figure of the Duke could be espied from the open pantry door as he entered the dining room.

'Fuck me,' Tom the footman said in a low whisper. 'Her Madge gone awol is what I heard, and the shoot today going ahead for all that...'

'But of course,' said Struthers gravely, heading for the dining room with his platter of eggs. He was thrown by the disappearance of the Queen; and he could have sworn the eggs winked up at him as he went, with their red eyes.

The Royal Escort

Austin Ford had been born and brought up in St Lucia, and, named after two makes of car imported to the island in his parents' youth, he liked to have printed on his card (which otherwise announced him as manager of 'The Escort Service', to be contacted at Windsor Village, Joli Plantation) a line drawing of a car, something like a Cadillac and certainly nothing like an Austin or a Ford. This was of no importance to Austin, or to his clients for that matter, as he did not own a car. A taxi could be got from the Joli Hilton rank if an outing to Soufrière, or to the nearest takeaway, was planned. Generally, however, the elderly ladies and occasional disorientated-looking men who called his mobile were happy to relax in Windsor Village, a half-built assortment of wooden Caribbean houses by the edge of the sea. Here was where the artificial white sand, supplied by the crushing of thousands of tons

69

of coral in order to fulfil the 'dream holiday' fantasy of guests of the hotel, ended and the indigenous black sand beach took over. Austin's customers did not ask to swim here, leaving a handful of Rastas to zoom up and down in rickety boats with a scarlet prow and a hideously noisy outboard engine. A 'King fish' (most fish on the hotel menu were called this) was occasionally speared in the hugely deep waters below the Piton and this was thrust instantly into the deep freeze of the not-quite-finished restaurant at Windsor Village. The Rum Shop, which Austin owned – he lived in a shack out the back and this was threatened with demolition, but letters to planning authorities took a year to receive an answer so its future was not yet known – stood next to the bamboo-gated entrance to the little enclave. A sill out in front meant they were never closed, though Austin sometimes pulled across an iron grille to prevent tourists from ransacking his supplies. It was from here today that he set out to meet and offer an escort service to the Queen.

Jolene was a frequent supplier of clients for her step-uncle's brother, Austin Ford. They had all grown up in the village above the Joli Estate and diversification had become vital when the future of the Windward island (bendy) banana was imperilled by the American straight banana and people saw they would have to struggle to survive. Austin had been the first to show enterprise, with the Rum

Shop, built from jetsam rescued from the sea after the increasingly frequent hurricanes and storms, but the locals preferred beer and the tourist season was so short – December till March – that the escort service had become a useful addition to Austin's income. For fifty US dollars, a visit to The Rum Shop and dinner in the almost-finished restaurant of local specialities such as jerk chicken (this had become famous amongst the sailors who flocked to the deep water of the bay and tied up to one of the bobbing white buoys there) could be followed by dancing (Jolene's younger sisters) and even, if booked well in advance, fire-eating and Highland reels. It was to a full evening's entertainment of this kind that Austin planned to invite Mrs Gloria Smith (Jolene had glimpsed the lady's passport when she checked in and saw slipped between the pages a photo of a strangely short-legged dog wearing a tartan overcoat and standing in the snow outside what looked like a fairy castle. There were clearly links with Scotland).

The kind of evening Austin had in mind, after receiving this information earlier, would take some time to bring to fruition. The cost would be one hundred US dollars. But he deserved a break: September was the very worst month in this part of the world, and a forewarning of Hurricane Bertie coming first to Tobago and then hammering Martinique and St Lucia made him all the more determined to make a good deal now while there was time. For tonight, Mrs Smith could enjoy a punch at The Rum Shop and maybe a takeaway from the Piton Grill if she would pay for the taxi. (The restaurant, as so often, was closed.) Austin also trusted that a deposit might be put down by Mrs Smith to pay for the skills employed by one of the island's most celebrated limbo dancers. Some of the regular visitors to Windsor Village, men who taught those on inclusive holidays at the Joli Hilton how to sail a catamaran or how to learn yoga while in the pool behind the Rainforest Bar, the tennis coaches and the masseurs, the workers who lived on the fringes of the tourist economy, would be invited to Mrs Smith's dinner party – which Austin now envisaged as taking up all of the first floor of the nearly-finished restaurant. A deposit would certainly be needed for so magnificent a reception. Austin's status would improve greatly. And Mrs Smith – who could tell? – might decide to buy a yacht and anchor permanently off Joli Bay.

With these intoxicating visions taking up his thoughts, Austin at first failed to recognise the small, snowy-haired woman who was just leaving the main door of the Joli Hilton as he walked up under palms towards it. But the description from Jolene was right – so if this was his new client, why had she not waited for him? Was she aware that what seemed an easy sloping road down to the beach was actually an exhausting effort for those from northern climes, in this heat? It was fortunate indeed that her escort, Mr Austin Ford – for now he bowed, took the lady's hand and introduced himself with great formality – had come just in time to prevent the consequences of walking all the way down.

The Queen, aka Mrs Gloria Smith, once she had firmly removed her hand from his, paid no more attention to Austin than she would to an equerry long in the royal household. A shuttle bus pulled up; and, indicating that she should mount and enter it, Austin was relieved that she did. It was only when the bus had stopped at Windsor Village and the new arrival at Joli Bay was ushered through the bamboo gate, that Austin Ford realised there was something missing in his client's get-up, for Mrs Smith, like any well-bred lady out for an evening stroll on her country estate, had not brought her handbag. And for a moment or two, Austin had no idea of what he should now do.

No Walkabout

The Queen had been quite surprised to find herself deserted by Austin Ford almost as soon as they stepped down from the shuttle bus and walked across a small stretch of artificial sand to the half-built houses by the sea. Used as she was to her name being used for all manner of pubs and un-suitable souvenirs, the words Windsor Village, inscribed on what was clearly a piece of flotsam washed up in a recent storm, seemed an unneces-sary reminder of the family – and in particular the Castle – which she had left on the other side of the world. She concentrated instead on the notice, clearly by the same signwriter, which proclaimed Rum Shop on the rickety building where she had been told to wait by the 'escort' provided. Like most of the equerries and courtiers she had known, Ford was someone with no idea of the needs of a royal personage: uncouth, unpleasantly smarmy, and on the verge of being totally uneducated, Austin Ford had not made a good first impression.

Now the sun sank in the sky with a rapidity to which the Queen was not accustomed. Apart from a single bulb hanging in the dining room of the nearly-finished restaurant, there would be no light soon. The Queen, feeling the wings of the first mosquito of the evening as it skimmed her cheek, began to fidget, a habit long ago trained out of her by the royal governess Crawfie – and, thinking for a moment of a far-distant childhood before Crawfie had dared to sell her innocent story to the press, the polite, firm girl she had been returned to show herself to the old lady abandoned here in an empty mock-village by a darkening sea. Where *was* one supposed to go next? Had her real identity been guessed: was this a horribly mismanaged walkabout? If so, where were the crush barriers and the balloons and streamers always present when there was a visit from the Queen? Austin Ford was more of an idiot than she had considered him to be.

While the sovereign pushed away a sudden longing for tea and crumpets with the dogs at Balmoral, she made a silent reminder to herself that her house would be built soon, even if its present appearance as no more than a hole in the ground was far from promising. Nothing had ever not been finished in time for the Queen, however inept or stupid those who constructed, repaired or drew architectural plans, happened to be. One way or another, a project had to be ready in time for the monarch's occupation, or for a royal visit: even if the building in question would be seen only once and then consigned to the lady-in-waiting's list of places called on and people seen there, it would, triumphantly new or refurbished, be ready for the Queen. Now at Windsor Village nothing was ready for her, there weren't even signs of preparation. And the escort, she had been informed by Jolene, would demand a deposit for his services to Mrs Gloria Smith (the Queen had reluctantly agreed and handed over ten dollars from the travel folder in her handbag). The escort or equerry or whatever he was had already vanished into thin air. It was all most unsatisfactory, especially as the Queen had paid a deposit through Westminster Travel for the house bought off-plan on the Joli Estate. Was this the new life the Queen had promised herself: a series of unrefundable deposits for a non-existent house and a disappeared escort? It was really too bad.

The Fate of the Handbag

Austin Ford was also suffering from feelings of extreme dissatisfaction. The fact of his client's coming down here for an evening out with no handbag (or any other visible sign of support: she clearly didn't have room in the pockets of the lavender tweed to stow a wallet and he very much doubted that dollar bills were tucked into her underwear) had led him to rush back to the Joli Hilton and demand of Jolene that she go with him to Mrs Smith's room to retrieve the white handbag. He had been a fool, of course, not to have noticed on the way down to the beach that Mrs Smith had no bag; but it was hard to think of a lady of that age without one, and it had simply not occurred to him that his new customer did not expect to incur expenses during an evening on the town (as Austin grandly put it to himself, even if nothing more than a takeaway was involved). Envisaging the worst, Austin reminded himself that he was the possessor of the ten-dollar note extracted from Mrs Smith by Jolene. Something grimly told him, however, that this was all he would see.

This turned out to be the case. Jolene gave a little shriek as they entered Room 209 and saw the shiny white bag lying on its side on the bed, clasps pulled rudely apart, and empty.

'Omigod!' said Jolene, who liked to copy the ridiculous things tourists on the beach came out with. 'Omi...'

'Passport, money, tickets,' Austin intoned. And it was true; the travel folder had gone, with its consignment of US dollars. There was no little purple fake-leather book with the royal coat of arms on the cover and there were no signs of a ticket which would enable Mrs Smith to leave the island when what Austin imagined to be her fortnight's 'inclusive' holiday was over.

'And the necklace!' Jolene cried. In rapid patois, she explained to Ford that she had seen the big, green stones in Mrs Smith's bag, and that there had been diamonds twinkling all round them.

'We go back down to the village,' announced Austin, as the (American) floor manager strolled past the room, paused and walked on.

Jolene carried the Queen's handbag on to the shuttle and down to a moonless sea. Only a nineteen-year-old girl on the bus had stared at the unlikely accessory – otherwise unmolested, Jolene and Ford slipped in the darkness down through the gate to find the Queen.

The Rainforest Bar

The beach at Joli Bay made for difficult walking, especially in the court shoes from the long-defunct shop in Bond Street where upper-class ladies were shod (in the Queen's case, of course, footwear was despatched to the palace for approval); and it was only when the first lights could be spotted through the thatched mini-huts and coconut fronds, these accompanied by large notices warning against falling coconuts and stern advice on swimming 'at your own risk' interspersed with the hulls of long-abandoned boats which proved particularly painful to the walker – it was only then, when it became possible to leave the edge of the sea and rise towards a long, glass building, that the way through became easier for the Queen. The lights grew more numerous and brighter as she approached: people could now be seen packed in behind the glass, and a door was open on to an AstroTurf lawn bordered by plumbago and tea roses.

'Who on earth is that?' A strident voice emanated from the Rainforest Bar of the Joli Hilton and the Queen stopped in her tracks. A spotlight and CCTV camera were trained on her – though she did not know this, all matters of security having been deliberately screened from her since her accession to the throne fifty-five years before – and a silence fell on the drinkers gathered round the bar and over-spilling into a marquee at the side which announced itself as 'Restaurant. Tonight's buffet: Latin.' Then the raucous party noise started up again: those who could see out on to the beach noticed only an elderly lady in a tweed suit which took the silver members of the holiday group back to the much-missed days of Norman Hartnell and Barbara Goalen; the rest, seeing there could be no danger involved, turned up the stereo and continued with the party mood.

'It is – yes it is –' said Sir Martyn Bostock, who could be seen by the Queen to be standing right up against the plate-glass window with his wife, frozen daiquiri in hand, at his side.

'That peculiar little woman who was on the plane. What on earth is she doing out there at this time of night?' demanded Lady Bostock. 'She's' – and here she tapped the side of her head and opened watery blue eyes very wide, as if to indicate madness. 'Don't you think we ought to tell someone?'

'Tell someone?' Sir Martyn pondered over a banana and Bacardi cocktail and shook his head. He didn't like to be reminded, when his wife made these accusations, of the streak of insanity in her own family, and he was forced to remember the time when his brother-in-law, owner of large swathes of Central London, had attempted to climb Nelson's column and had had to be locked up for several weeks in the Priory.

'Leave well alone,' Sir Martyn advised.

But management, warned about the CCTV camera, was now picking its way through the revellers, and huge security spotlights lit up the beach and artificial garden just outside the Rainforest Bar. The Queen, blinded at first, made her way instinctively towards the window where she had seen Sir Martyn clear as day, and his dotty wife, before the alarm went up. 'Arise Sir Martyn!' A vague picture of the House of Commons and then of a sewage works in somewhere like Reading, came to mind. But surely, now his monarch needed him, he would help her gain entry to the Rainforest Bar and then on to a shuttle back to the main portion of the Joli Hotel. A knight in shining armour he might not be, but...

The Queen had never been shut out of a place before. Had she wished it, she could visit every stately home in Great Britain and be accorded the most rapturous and respectful welcome. High security prisons, the inner enclosures at the most exclusive racecourses, four-star restaurants with waiting lists of several years would all fling open their doors for her. (Possibly, only White's Club in St James's would demur at permitting the reigning sovereign to enter their portals. But this was probably due more to anti-Hanoverian sentiment on the part of the dukes and ancient lines of earls and the rest who were members of the club and not due to the Queen's gender. As it stood, she could change neither her genetic provenance nor her sex.)

For the Queen suffered the humiliation of walking right up to the glass door, only to find it closed in her face. Worse, in her long experience of doors opened by bowing flunkeys, she had no way of dealing with this unexpected snub. She walked on – and, like a child outside a sweet shop, found her nose pressed up against the plate glass. Management, in the shape of three dark-suited personnel – two men and a woman – opened the door a crack and slipped out to interrogate the Queen.

Saving the Queen

Austin Ford and Jolene, after exploring the interior of The Rum Shop (but it was most unlikely, they both knew, that the respectable Mrs Smith had been boozing in their absence and had fallen unconscious in there) – and once they realised that Windsor Village had no occupant at present – set off across the beach. Ford had a regular job after sundown every evening – but a curiosity about his client drove him to make for the Rainforest Bar: he had her handbag with him, for one thing, and a feeling of compassion and sadism mixed made him wonder what she would do when she discovered it had been emptied of all that was valuable, in her absence. Why the old lady had left her hotel room door open was one of the unanswerable questions pertaining to Mrs Smith: Jolene said it was like Auntie May's dementia where she never recognised people and forgot dates; Austin, puzzled on a deeper level,

95

thought maybe the elderly Englishwoman had escaped from an institution. But then how did she manage to get to St Lucia? It was all very baffling.

The Rainforest Bar had fewer drinkers than earlier: no one liked to be reminded by the dark-suited presence of security personnel that this 'dream holiday' was actually set on an island where terrible poverty and vastly wealthy yacht and villa owners mingled little. The trained friendliness of Joli Hotel staff, once they had disembarked from the shuttle carrying native islanders down from their poky accommodation high up the valley (guests travelled in buses containing all white passengers) convinced many of those staying at the hotel that a happy relationship between staff and visitor was possible: that this might have a false and over-optimistic bias reminded Joli clientele of the reality of life here. So when Austin and Jolene strolled up to the plate-glass windows of the bar, it was possible to see a thinning crowd. There was a sense of restlessness and displeasure at the intrusion – as they saw it – of a suspicious person such as the old lady outside trying to gatecrash an evening of salsa dancing followed by a Latin buffet in the marquee beyond the bar. People streamed out, to wait for a shuttle that would take them to the taxi rank outside the main reception. Soufrière might have its shabbiness and its dangers – but there was a hotel there where inclusive holidaymakers were catered for and most of the hotel guests decided to go to the Hummingbird, thus losing restaurant and bar a considerable sum of money.

Only one couple lingered by the glass door; a late middle-aged couple Austin had never seen before, and therefore new arrivals at the Joli Hotel. He hoped they might be friends of Mrs Smith – although he doubted this: she seemed an independent sort and he was surprised she had agreed to the escort service in the first place. Besides this, the lady was staring out through the now guarded glass door with an expression of disgust on her face. And it was because the subject of Security's investigations was of such modest stature that Austin, seeing the gaze now transferring to the husband of the couple, had to assume a haughty air – most of the guards were cousins and understood Austin's facial comments on a situation – and push past Security to save his client.

Mrs Gloria Smith showed neither surprise nor gratitude at Austin Ford's rescue; nor, as the dark-suited brigade moved away, did she acknowledge the sudden restoration of her white handbag from Jolene. She took the bag, in fact, as if she had only temporarily set it down somewhere and was unsurprised to see it back on her arm.

Austin was stymied by this reaction. Surely, any normal person would thank him effusively, and then open the bag in eagerness, hoping to find they had not been robbed.

Nothing like that, however, from Mrs Smith.

What was he to do? Jolene, maybe, could refer to the fact that the hotel room had been left unlocked and therefore it was best to check if money, passport and valuables were still inside. But Jolene hung back too – while a cut-glass voice demanded to return to the Joli Hotel. Mrs Smith's precise and clear accents wafted in to where that same couple stood, drinks untouched in their hands, still staring out as if they'd both seen the same ghost.

'Non Joli,' Austin said. How could he explain to Mrs Smith that without money – a deposit, again, came into it – there was no way reception would allow this luggage-less and empty-handbagged woman to spend the night.

'Nonsense,' came the reply. 'One would like one's dinner now and there seem to be no signs of it in the – in Windsor Village.'

There was nothing for it but to inform his client that dinner would be served in the Rum Shop, premises which belonged exclusively to Austin Ford. A bed could be made up for later and a curtain hung in the shack, for propriety.

'I go and get you pizza,' Austin said. He had the ten dollars she had given Jolene, and that was it: September was a terrible month. 'And a rum punch,' said Austin. He decided to throw this in for free: tomorrow at dawn he would go and find that couple who had been staring at Mrs Smith from the bar, and demand they take her to the Consul – or the airport – or the Police. He could give no more time to a woman who couldn't even open her handbag and was like Auntie May, quite mad.

Pizza or Burger

The Queen had to wait longer for her pizza than she had ever waited for a meal. There had been a delay in Rome and another at the Elysée Palace when the ortolans had had to be called off after a furious missive from the British Ambassador. The Queen, it was pointed out, would absolutely not be prepared to bury her head in a paper bag as she ate the prized – and illegal – bird; nor would she follow the habit of scoffing them down, bones and all, in one long mouthful, followed by a swig of Armagnac. There had been panic in the kitchens and thrushes were substituted – by then the Embassy was too fraught to complain and it was agreed that the menu should describe the course as 'baby quails'. It had all taken ages and the disapproval on the royal features was only too evident. Coming after another unpleasant bulletin on the subject of Britain's lack of a written constitution, this French insistence on forbidden (and probably disgusting) food had brought on a couple of tactless and bad-tempered remarks from the Duke, and a decision on the part of the Queen to refuse the European Union for as long as she could. She had stood out against hereditary titles and estates going to female children (in the case of the monarchy it was different; there were no male heirs at the time of her accession – this she knew, although a tiresome genealogist wrote his article about searching for a pretender every ten years or so but no one paid any attention) and now, after seeing the suppressed laughter on the faces of the footmen at the circulating story about Mitterand and his way of eating the banned little birds, the Queen had left all the fine wines set down in front of her, untouched: a veritable insult to France.

Here in St Lucia she was in a very different situation – but the pangs of hunger were reminiscent of that awful evening in Paris a few years back. She had never known real hunger, of course; but this wait for Austin to bring the promised fast food (they might be out of pizza and if so he'd return with a burger, he had said before setting off on an old bicycle kept for journeys after the shuttle up to the hotel had stopped running). The Queen hoped it would not be a burger – she hadn't tried a pizza, although she had heard an ex-daughter-in-law warning her girls to keep off them and this had made them sound appetising – but soon almost anything would be welcome, as visions of Austin pedalling slowly up the hill and even into Soufrière to fetch her supper became increasingly frequent.

A moon had finally risen over the sea, and noting a large yacht with striped funnels like a children's book illustration as it came slowly gliding in to tie up at one of the buoys further down the beach, the Queen decided for the second time that evening to leave the dark and deserted Windsor Village and make her way back to company and civilization. Surely, the security personnel so efficiently despatched by Ford would not return – and the odious Bostocks must by now have decided to sit down to dinner. The Queen decided not to think about this. She had no idea what a Latin buffet could be, but she would be willing to try it. And soon, as she walked in the now-painful Charles Jourdain shoes across the crushed coral beach, the Queen realised that this was why she was making for the Rainforest Bar once more: for the first time in her life she was famished, and even if it meant sampling the 'real seafood soup' she had seen an elderly inclusive tourist bringing to his wife's table (Heinz tomato, even the Queen could see this was what it was), all the failures and disappointments of the day would be forgotten and gone. She was grateful to Austin Ford for his efforts to bring her dinner down through the hot night on the handlebars of a bicycle, she could even feel that he was not so disastrous in his attempt to be her equerry as she had at first imagined. But to rely on someone like that for bed and board: this was a ridiculous notion. Of course the Joli Hotel would see to it that she had her room back, once she had dined. There was no doubt in the Queen's mind that there was nothing to worry about and that everything would turn out all right.

The Old Man in the Sea

It would be hard to say which now came first – the Queen seeing something bobbing about in the sea under a moon suddenly out and blazing silver-white down on a beach responding in brightness, or the figure in the water seeing her and ducking and diving, arms raised, to escape possible recognition or capture. The Queen had stumbled – this on emerging from the Rainforest Bar where security was still very much in force, and a slightly frosty (why were they taking so long?) demand for a table had been met by a grim insistence she open her white handbag and give proof both of her identity and evidence of travellers' cheques or US dollars. The Queen had suffered one further humiliation of being asked to hand over her bag; and on refusing to accede to this request she had had it confiscated, opened by Security (who was posing as a waiter) and the full extent of its emptiness was revealed.

Only an ancient tissue was pulled from the recesses of the Queen's shiny handbag: this provided by Lady Lettice Farquhar at the time of a Britannia cruise up past the Castle of Mey before joining the royal train to Balmoral. Now, on this far-distant shore, the ancient paper handkerchief fell limply to the floor of the Rainforest Bar; and the Queen, finding herself ejected by the management of the Joli Hotel, turned and walked down the beach, where a forgotten deck chair tripped her up and caused her almost – but not quite – to lose her balance and fall. It was then, righting herself and walking firmly on, that the Queen spotted the human or animal in the deep waters near the Piton: white, with an abundance of long white hair and a white hairiness over arms and chest which reminded the Queen of the Scottish fairy tales of an old man said to live in the hills. The Loch Ness Monster could scarcely equal the oddness of this apparition – but the Queen, who did not suffer from fear, and had seen it only on the faces of people brought to meet her, stood quite unmoved on the beach and stared until the creature dived down out of sight and swam away.

It was then that the Queen saw in the moonlight that Austin Ford also stood by the edge of the sea, about a hundred yards from where she was. He also stared out at the dark, calm water; and he held a white towelling robe in his arms

'Who was that, Ford?' The icy accents of Mrs

Gloria Smith brought a mumbled apology from Austin; and as she grew nearer, she heard that the pizza place had been closed and he had stopped and bought her a bag of nuts.

Only when he had been asked two more times who or what this nocturnal visitor to the Joli Bay might be, did Austin, still ungracious to the client of his escort service, give his reply. He pulled a pale and tasteless cashew from the Queen's small plastic bag and thrust it into his mouth. The answer, therefore, was indistinct; and as no one had ever spoken to the Queen with their mouth full, a silence ensued.

'The King,' Austin said, before setting off to his home in the half-finished village.

He looked behind him only once. The old lady could hardly be left out all night – she should not have set out again and Austin Ford resolved she must be dealt with as soon as day broke. On his surprising response to her question, his client made no comment at all.

A New Roof

The Queen spent an uncomfortable night on the camp bed in Austin Ford's shack – this concealed from curious eyes in the Rum Shop by a tired-looking floral curtain and a tottering pile of crates which had clearly been her new equerry's inspiration: his client deserved privacy and this was almost a wall.

Despite these attentions, the Queen could not get to sleep. Moonlight came in knife-shaped patterns through the outer planking of the hut. Mosquitoes danced maddeningly out of reach and always ready to return. And images of the amphibian snowy-haired man glimpsed earlier in the sea rose before her eyes in a mist as pervasively white and painful as the migraine the Queen had once suffered at a tribal display in South Africa. That this blinding headache came from the fact of having eaten the bag of nuts Ford had brought back from his trip to

Soufrière, the Queen was certain: the nuts had been salty in the extreme, and Her Majesty's diet had excluded salt on medical advice for many years. There was also – and this she could not admit, as the royal lips had sipped so cautiously over the span of her reign that it was said there was no one in the realm who could make a glass of wine last as long as the Queen – there was, too, the probability of the head and eye trouble being, quite simply, a hangover. But of course the monarch could not recognise the symptoms. All she knew was that the old man in the sea, the whine of the circling insects and the jagged slices of bright light on the floor and walls of the shack equalled nothing the Queen had ever experienced. So she made no objection when a couple of knuckles knocked against a crate in the makeshift room divider and Austin looked round to check on his guest

'What is it, Ford?' The Queen sat bolt upright on the rickety truckle, the old ex-Army blanket with which she had been provided now tickling her chin and adding to the severe discomfort she already suffered. 'What time is it? When will it be light? There appears to be no clock here and one would like one provided, please. And bring me a glass of water, if you would be so good. Thank you.'

Austin Ford said it would be night for a long time yet. He went behind the crates and pulled a plastic bottle labelled Piton Water – but actually filled at the standpipe used by the builders at

Windsor Village – and handed it to his eccentric client, Mrs Gloria Smith. He had to admire the way the old lady, who clearly had never swigged from a bottle before, raised it to her lips after looking round and silently noting the absence of a glass; and he wondered just where she had been incarcerated all these years. People wanted to emigrate to Britain from here and other islands, Austin knew, but when they came back to visit relatives they told dreadful tales of prisons and hospitals – and lunatic asylums too, where those who had not adapted to the British way of life found themselves consigned. The question remained, though: how and why did Mrs Smith come to St Lucia? Austin was determined to find out. She could be friendly, old Mrs Smith, if she wanted to be, and yesterday evening's rum punches, extra sweetened with the sickly pink grenadine to counter the effect of the nuts (there had been complaints about the salt content) had brought tales of her dogs, and Christmas in the snow in Scotland – and even a confession, almost lachrymose, that an adored governess had been badly treated once she was no longer needed by the family. 'She sees us every day when we drive past her bungalow...' but here the sad story had ended. Austin wondered if the subject of this past governess would be a good way to get at the truth about the mysterious Mrs Smith. Pulling a crate to the centre of the makeshift room, he sat down, elbows on knees, and took on a friendly posture. After all,

Jolene had spoken of green stones and twinkling stones in Mrs Smith's empty handbag: if they were real, this must be urgently investigated. Had Mrs Smith run away from a mad people's home, counting on the jewels to fund her in her blind rush out of the UK? It was the wrong time of night to suggest more alcohol – and poor Mrs Smith, who now gasped in horror at the taste of the chemical-laden water in the plastic bottle, seemed quite unused to the modest amount with which he had plied her earlier. So what could loosen her tongue? Austin reached out and pulled a fly swatter from its hiding place in the hammered-together deadwood outer wall of the Rum Shop. Two mosquitoes fell dead on the floor when he swatted them and the Queen clapped her hands together in delight. 'Well done, Ford,' came in high, crystalline tones. Austin thought of mad Auntie May and her ancient wireless, and for a second a picture of a plum pudding with a twig of frangipani poked in it came into his mind.

The Queen was also thinking hard about her next move. It had been a shock, discovering at the Rainforest Bar that her jewels had disappeared. Francis Teck may have been a bit of a bounder, but he'd been the brother-in-law of Queen Mary, the Queen's grandmother, after all, and it was a heinous crime to steal the Cambridge emeralds (the Queen was unsure whether the stones belonged to the State or to her: this was a common confusion when it came to real estate, Old Masters, jewellery and the rest, and was one of the reasons for the demand that royal ownership of treasures and palaces be clarified).

The Queen wondered how she could persuade Austin Ford to search for the missing stones. It did not occur to her that her new escort would need little persuading. But now he was talking – telling her about his family, it seemed, with words of a wife and a former wife and their children up in the village, and the trip they planned to take in a private plane to Mustique (when he had found the emeralds, Austin did not add).

The Queen was an expert listener. Of all the hundreds and thousands of family confidences she had received in her long years on the throne she remembered in particular one point: there was always a moment when the teller, over-emotional at being granted a royal audience, mentioned the one grudge – or crime – or stain of illegitimacy, which continued to haunt them and would do so for the rest of their days. Obviously, Ford couldn't know that his client Mrs Smith was the Queen of England – but she had perfected the art of listening to a stage where not coming out with some kind of confession seemed to the teller to be a crime in itself. 'So the rest of your family went to live in Australia,' the Queen said, and an image of cheering crowds came to her so she smiled gently. 'And I suppose you must miss them terribly, Ford?'

But Ford as well was proficient in the art of extracting information from unwary speakers. '*You* tell me,' he said. 'I don't know where you from, Gloria!' And he felt for some reason ashamed of his sudden familiarity with the old lady.

But the Queen knew the mechanics of the snub as well as encouragement and apparent interest. 'One has come a long way and one has had a tiring day,' came the answer. 'But one *is* rather intrigued by that, that man in the sea this evening. An expatriate, one imagines. How long has he lived here? You said, if I remember correctly, that he is a Mr King...'

'No,' said Ford, who saw now that intimacies would not be forthcoming. 'He the King, that what I say.' These were Austin's last words, for he saw his guest, on hearing this, shake her head and smile. Then her eyes closed and she sank down on to the hard bed.

A Cup of Tea

When morning finally came, the Queen woke from a dream of two of her corgis, Whisky and Sherry, jumping on her bed as in the morning they always did; and then, surfacing further from a patchy sleep, she could have sworn she heard the precise tones of her maid Ivy, bringing in tea, saying good morning before setting down the Tupperware box containing scones and fancy biscuits, which the sovereign and her dogs invariably shared.

But the heavy weight that descended on the Queen turned out to be a large, unappetising fruit in a cardboard box. A rusty knife lay beside it. Austin Ford had clearly thought of breakfast for his client; but the sight of the custard-yellow collapsed football (as in the perception of the Queen this tropical fruit resembled) brought an even stronger urge for tea and she rose resolutely and walked out of the small shack into bright sunlight. There was

no Miss Struthers standing in the half-built village
(she was the Queen's private secretary at Balmoral)
to discuss the day's events; there was, the Queen
knew perfectly well, no schedule set out for her for
the rest of her days. But it was hard to do without
one, and she determined to start the morning with
a visit to the site of No. 5 Bananaquit Drive high in
the Joli valley above the hotel and guest cottages.
There would be a contractor waiting for her on
site, surely; maybe even the architect of the Joli
development would make a point of coming down
from the capital, Castries, to discuss the construc-
tion of the home she had bought off-plan and to
apologise for and explain the delay. Tea would be
found at reception: the maid Jolene could provide
it and she could unlock the door of the little shop
in the foyer while she was about it. The Queen
wanted clean clothes in a light material: she might
even take a straw hat she had seen hanging on a
hook behind the boutique door.

That she would be unable to pay for these items
did not cross the Queen's mind. She would make a
telephone call from the lobby to Brno in Romania
where he was buying property for himself as well as
overseeing the Prince of Wales's new house and
eco-inspired land there – and Brno would telegraph
the money to the monarch whose patronage had
enabled him to prosper in a new environment without owing the Exchequer any payment at all. The
Queen knew about wiring funds – the Duke of

Windsor had been an ardent admirer of Western Union – and she imagined the funds would arrive when she had ordered her tea and selected summer wear at the shop.

The Queen walked barefoot to the far end of the beach: the court shoes were unwearable by now, due to a broken heel on one shoe and a snapped strap on the other; and she waited by a sign which again warned her to beware of falling coconuts, for the shuttle up to reception. Sure enough, as if Miss Struthers had indeed organised the transport for the first lady of the realm (and daughter of the head of the British Empire in its last days), a bus appeared almost at once, carrying staff down from a high-up village to prepare food and clean the Rainforest Bar and pool. The Queen, espying Jolene amongst them, gave a regal wave, and found herself asked to wait for a guests' shuttle to take her up the hill; but – as she gave the impression no one had ever refused her anything before – there was no stopping the indomitable Mrs Smith from boarding the bus and taking the front seat. With the mysterious visitor as its solitary passenger, the shuttle groaned slowly up under the palms to reception.

The scene there was quite unexpected, for it was still early morning in the Caribbean. The first thing the Queen noticed was the large number of people in the foyer – it was impossible to get to the desk or, as they were all apparently English or American and therefore taller than she, to see over or round them to find the concierge. An outing had been arranged for the Joli guests, the Queen supposed; but she feared that ordering tea would be out of the question for a long time. Then it occurred to her that they might be all going back – home – as she still must consider England to be. Would a coach come for them soon and make it possible to get on with her day?

But now the Queen saw that all these residents – or tourists – or guests – at the Joli Hotel were staring in one direction, and a silence had fallen as an announcer's voice boomed out from the sitting area on the far side of reception. The TV was positioned there; and as she picked her way through the crowd, the Queen saw Sir Martyn and Lady Bostock standing close up by the desk, their faces purple with excitement, and the concierge plucking at their sleeves and mouthing questions. The Queen pressed on until a hugely tall man, a tennis coach with JOLI printed in towering letters on his T-shirt, almost crushed the old lady determinedly sidling through the crowd.

'I beg your pardon, ma'am.' The coach was American: the Queen understood this, while registering that the correct way of addressing a female royal personage had been used for the first time since her arrival on the island. 'Let me assist you, ma'am.' The coach had seen that the dignified-looking woman was barefoot, of all things... Who and what could she be?

The Queen reached the TV at last, and if it had not been for nearly three quarters of a century's practice in her role as Head of State she would, like the crowd gathered in reception of the Joli Hotel in St Lucia, have cried out in astonishment at what she saw.

Hyde Park – it obviously *was* Hyde Park – and then, unmistakably, came the gates of Buckingham Palace, camera panning out to take in the length of the Mall – everywhere showed blown-up posters of the Queen, pictured against a vast array of floral tributes and these tied to railings and laid reverentially on every spare inch of grass. The image of Her Majesty dominated the screen. A newsreader repeated endlessly the unbelievable truth that the monarch of the realm had departed from her palace and her throne. Stifled sobs could be heard in the crowded foyer of the hotel, while shouts and weeping fits attracted cameramen at the scene.

The Queen slipped out of the glass door and into the circular driveway; and, grateful for the palms standing on a triangle of over-sprinkled grass there, she escaped unseen down a side path to the distant sea.

The People's Queen

The Queen missed the way from reception at the Joli Hotel down to the lots for sale, and after circling the middle and lower reaches of the lush estate where her house at Bananaquit Drive must surely be, she gave up the idea of meeting the builders – as she had hoped – on site, and decided to make for the Rainforest Bar. Here, despite the bad manners shown by management last night, she would surely be able to order tea (Earl Grey if possible) and make a plan involving Austin Ford and a car to take her to buy clothes and shoes in Soufrière. As she had never arranged transport or shopping herself, it was not possible to foresee difficulty; and although she was aware she had been robbed and her handbag was as empty as even the most arduous lady-in-waiting would have liked, the Queen assured herself that Brno would be on the other end of the line when she called – for she had never in all her fifty-five years on the throne been asked to 'hang on' or – worse – been offered several 'options' to determine the nature of her inquiry.

It would be hard to say that even a royal person-age trained to exhibit no feelings, and to react to even the most outrageous situations (war, divorce of children, abdication of uncle, accession to the throne) with calm and a total absence of emotion, could go for long without betraying their inner thoughts on the TV news footage just ingested by the Queen. Her people loved her! She was, presum-ably, considered dead and mourned for having retained precisely that monumental calm in the face of a usurper (as she considered the late Princess of Wales to have been) or terrorist attacks – or even at Diana's death the demand she lower the flag at Buckingham Palace – and this after having to agree to pay tax for the first time in the recent history of the monarchy! She was now proved, in her absence, to be the people's Queen. The people might have refused to pay for the restoration of Windsor Castle after the fire, but they admired and loved their monarch and wanted her safely back where she belonged, on the throne.

Despite the self-control instilled throughout her childhood, the Queen was unable to prevent herself from giving a shy smile when the realisation of her popularity began to sink in. But, as she had so often been taught when young, thinking of yourself leads to muddle and to vanity: and it was thus, pleasantly confused, that she missed the road where the shuttles drove, and, taking a footpath that soon petered out in thick rainforest, was soon totally lost

The sea glittered below; trees, bearing a pink blossom that appeared to fall and then renew itself as she walked under them, arched below giant creepers. Little bursts of rain lasted no more than a minute before a hot sun struggled once more to penetrate the undergrowth. Twice, the Queen stumbled on the root of an unrecognisable tree. But the vision of the sea, postcard blue and capped with tiny white waves, drew her on and down. This must be the coast below: here she would find the Rainforest Bar – or, if she arrived at Windsor Village, there she would find Ford and he would bring her tea. For the Queen, like all who have employed servants, saw all those inferior to her in class and status as potential doers of the royal bidding.

'Madam.' The voice was gruff and appeared to issue from behind a large boulder on the forest path. 'You are mistaking your way, madam,' the voice continued, as its owner came heavily up through a cleared area: behind him, as the Queen could now see, the land dropped away steeply and what appeared to be a monastery or abbey sat further down, its colonnades pointing out to sea.

'Where is one?' said the Queen. She had recognised the old man with flowing white hair as the creature glimpsed in the sea off Joli Beach, Ford in attendance with a towel.

'Ravissant Estate,' replied the old man.

The Queen waited. There would surely be an invitation to go down to the religious-looking building below, which, as she now saw, had a gold roof. Possessor of unlimited amounts of art treasures, castles and palaces, the Queen felt no particular interest in the building – although thoughts of a boring film about Tibet shown her by Prince Charles did come to mind. 'May one follow you down?' the Queen asked the old man.

But no invitation was forthcoming. Despite his age, the King (as the Queen had heard him called by Ford, and for that reason she felt she would like to know more about him) descended with agility to his demesne overlooking the sea.

The Queen had never not been invited by anyone before. Her subjects were warned months in advance of the royal arrival and departure dates, and were presumed to be grateful for the information. No, the present Queen had never been rejected in this way before. Surprised at this rebuff from the white-haired recluse, she decided she must find Ford urgently, and a path that would lead away from the forested kingdom of the old man.

The sea grew nearer as she walked and half slithered down the side of the Piton where she had lost her way. Then the Queen found herself almost at once just above the half-finished village which bore her name.

The Rum Shop

'So that's two banana daiquiris, three Piton lagers and a Coke,' said the tourist to the woman behind the bar of the Rum Shop – this newly opened with wooden sill extended to provide a counter-cum-bar, and on the floor a nest of stools for those too old, tired or drunk to stay on their feet.

That this was frequently the case for the customers of Austin Ford's 'internationally famous' establishment (announced on the reverse of the Escort Service card along with a line drawing of a cocktail glass topped with a cherry) was confirmed by today's batch of drinkers in the half-finished village. With a combined age of at least three centuries, the white-haired or egg-bald Canadian gentlemen, their wives in long caftans and dangling earrings hanging by the sides of their faces in an attempt to conceal jowls or wrinkles, the customers at the Rum Shop – with the exception of a solitary American male – were all

Commonwealth born and reared. That their monarch, the Queen of Canada's snowy wastes, the sovereign of high-rise cities and pine-clad mountains, leader of all those banished from a cruel homeland ruled over by kings uncaring of the Clearances and bored at the thought of this distant offshoot of Scotland far away – that this historic personage was the one who served the drinks here today, would have been surprising in the extreme to them. A tour of 'Wild St Lucia', comprising a brief walk in the botanical gardens and a goggle down at the sulphur springs which gave Soufrière its name, followed by a handiwork shop in the town and the purchase of miniature wooden boats, further dangly earrings and postcards of the Pitons, meant that no one had seen TV all day; and thus the news of the disappearance (or possible demise) of the Queen was unknown to the group. The Rum Shop had no television; it had been billed as a more 'authentic' visit to a St Lucian village than the Rainforest Bar or the Joli Hotel could provide.

The Queen had demonstrated her usual pragmatic good sense when Austin, determined to go off fishing in the deep waters beyond the Gros Piton, greeted her on her return from her visit to reception and subsequent adventures in the wilds of 'the King's' secret land, with the information that he was leaving now and would be out all day. 'Auntie', as he now called this strange new client, must mind the bar. Go easy with the grenadine, put rum in the coke and say it's a Crack Baby cocktail... Austin, unaware that he addressed the woman who had granted him and all St Lucians independence when he was a child, lingered a little longer by the bar. Then, with a shout to the Rasta revving up his broken outboard engine at the end of the beach, he strode off to embark on his day's fishing.

The Queen by now realised that further visits to the Rainforest Bar were not advisable. She would either be evicted, as had happened already, or recognised – and there was no way of knowing which was worse. The memory of Lady Bostock's excited face floated before her as she assured this unusually wilful servant (no permission had been asked for him to go out in a boat all day; this surely could never happen at Balmoral) of her acquiescence to his request. But by the time she granted him leave, Ford had gone. The Queen knew it was her duty to repay the proprietor of the Rum Shop in some way, for, dimly at first and then with certainty, she realised that she depended on him to help her avoid the global outcry already seen underway on Sky News at the hotel. Austin could hide her. And, as she went firmly into the Rum Shop, fighting a wave of nausea at the sickly sweet smell of alcohol and days-old flat Coke there, she prepared to do her duty; she did not yet, but this would come along with the thirsty Canadians, give thought to the fact that she had no option other than to trust that strangers would show her the same degree of kindness that she, in those already far-off days when she had been Head of State, had happily shown them.

High Noon

By noon, when the sun had taken a new and menacing strength, the Queen decided she would leave the Rum Shop and go across to the half-finished restaurant to see if any meals were to be served today. It seemed an age since Austin had set out – the phut-phut of the engine had ceased abruptly once the boat arrived by the great dark bulk of the Gros Piton: it had broken down but she was not to know this, and it was possible that a good catch would galvanise the cook into action. This she fervently hoped: the tourists, now the worse for wear after drinking in this heat, would otherwise have to walk the length of the beach to the Rainforest Bar and there was of course no guarantee that they would get anything to eat once there. Booked into a humble boarding house where the shriek of incoming jets was their twenty-four-hour entertainment, they had clearly set out without even the minimum breakfast – and not one looked as if the 'inclusive' menu, 'real seafood soup' or even Latin buffet, would be on offer to them there. The Queen was not considered to be a person who felt pity or compassion for others – she was hardly deemed to be a person, after all, she was the Queen – but she did feel strangely sorry for her elderly Canadian subjects as they huddled under a canopy on benches by the edge of the rock-strewn sea. How patient these people were! – and the Queen thought of the probable reaction of any of her children (or the Duke) to finding themselves hungry and sunburned, with no food in sight. Would they have taken such an appalling mistake on the part of the organisers (for the Queen assumed every event to be meticulously organised and did not realise that the tourists would have received merely an email ticket and a brief print-out of places to eat and drink in St Lucia) – would anyone she knew show the patience and good humour of these people?

The probable answer was that the sole member of the Windsor family capable of forbearance in trying circumstances was the Queen. She did not like the way her trip and new home had turned out – but, in all the previous catastrophes, she had shown she could put up with anything, or almost anything. It just seemed unfair that retirement appeared to herald another *annus horribilis*, this time in a most uncomfortable heat. But this was not on a par with worrying about her grandson William and the break-up of his romance, or Harry, with his resolve to get himself shot at by a sniper in the Middle East. No, the Queen would put up with it here. If she had a desire to go home, it was only because the dogs must miss her so much. But she was not of a sentimental nature. Now she must serve a man in his thirties or forties who had just arrived at the half-finished Windsor Village on foot. This was a more prosperous-looking tourist than the rest: he had an expensive camera slung round his neck and wore shorts that were distinctly a cut above the gear worn by the others. The Queen, hot and weary as she was, went back to the Rum Shop and stood by the counter. This was her duty: it would be helpful to Ford.

'A banana daiquiri?' the Queen asked, her precise tones causing heads to turn at the long refectory tables by the sea. The new visitor did not reply to this and the Queen went on, but with a trace of uncertainty this time in her voice: 'A Crack Baby cocktail? A rum punch?'

But the camera had been taken from round the just-arrived customer's neck and the lens, the round black void of glass which was all the Queen had known of intimate relations with the outside world, was now trained on her, unfaltering, speeding its images for the world to see.

'Just stand there and smile, little lady,' the man

said, laughing. (He was an American, definitely not a subject, the Queen decided). 'That's a great shot, honey. I'll go for a beer.'

The Bar

It had been a long, hot day and by the time the sun was sinking with its usual speed over the great flat blank of the sea, the Queen decided to close the Rum Shop and lie down at the back of the hut on the truckle bed. The Canadian tourists had gone some hours before, to be replaced by a contingent of American female professors and a couple of English women who demanded gin and tonics and became petulant when it was explained to them that this was a rum shop.

'Or just neat gin,' insisted the younger of the pair of superannuated ex-debutantes (the Queen recognised them for what they were: possibly the elder was Boofy's girl, and had enjoyed drinking gin in the Royal Beach Hut at Sandringham years ago). 'What kind of a bar *is* this, for God's sake?' And, turning to her companion, she wondered aloud whether the 'King' in his secret estate behind the Petit Piton, would welcome a visit at this hour.

'Too early,' the younger agreed. The Queen saw that a Hermès headscarf circa 1961 fluttered from a shorts' pocket. Heavens! Was this... Fiona... that girl Charles had almost married, before it was clear she could never get up for early service at Crathie? Now who on earth *was* Fiona? It was one of those big Anglo-Irish families... She looked half asleep now, if you came to think of it.

'I'll settle for a fruit punch, no point in visiting the King and being so drunk you forget to ask to see the emeralds,' Boofy's girl announced. 'It'd pay off the mortgage, the ring he slipped on my finger a couple of years ago.'

'Well, he slipped it off again,' Fiona joked.

The Queen felt almost nostalgic, for the talk of gin made her think of the Queen Mother and the reminders of a lost era inspired by the handsome horse, depicted in colour on the silk Hermès scarf, brought pictures of Bond Street and then of the royal jeweller's, Wartski, where that terribly nice man would drop everything if summoned to the Palace to discuss the resetting of an item in the monarch's glittering array of jewels. Then she thought of the Cambridge emeralds, and how they had disappeared almost as soon as she arrived on the island. What would Her Late Majesty Queen Mary have thought of the present Queen's carelessness – or had the scandal of Francis of Teck and his mistress been kept from her? The truth would never be known, and the Queen felt terribly tired; serving the American women who, eyeing their British upper-class contemporaries with ill-concealed disgust, now clustered by the wooden sill of the bar, was the very last thing she wanted to do. For the Queen would find it effortless to make conversation with Boofy's girl or Fiona – but the... what were they? the Queen did not choose, like her great-grandmother Queen Victoria, to forbid the existence of lesbians; but to these unappetising and strident women she could think of nothing whatever to say. Besides, one of these monsters was speaking of 'empowerment' and other meaningless but threatening terms were bandied about by the sisters, most of whom were unkempt in the extreme.

'No,' – the voice the Queen refused them with was crystalline and startled both of the English visitors, so they looked hard at the woman behind the bar and then subsided again into their fruit punches, topped up with grenadine – 'no, there is no Bourbon here.' And then, recovering from the unpleasant after-effect of pronouncing the name of the guillotined Royal Family of France, the Queen pulled up the sill and marched to the back of the hut.

'What an odd woman,' Boofy's girl's voice sounded through the badly nailed-together planks.

'Yes, apparently they go bushy if they stay out in

the tropics too long,' the owner of the Hermès headscarf concurred. 'But I'm sure she wasn't here a couple of years ago when I came on Roman's yacht...'

But by the time Fiona had embarked on her reminiscences of her last trip to the island, the Queen had fallen fast asleep.

Secrets

Now, darkness had come and a swelling moon climbed the sky. Austin Ford and the Queen sat in companionable silence on the beach, the Queen in a pair of new flip-flops purchased for her by Austin in Soufrière on his return from his fishing trip (he had caught a fish and had sold it to the Rainforest Bar immediately – and just as quickly it had been thrown into the deep freeze, to emerge at some future date as a creature suitable for a Latin, Italian or American buffet – or as one of the unidentifiable components of an 'island barbecue' at an inclusive Saturday night).

'You know, I think I take you to my village so you meet my Auntie May,' Austin was saying. 'Tomorrow, maybe. And we go to find that Lot 75 man, that builder, and I make him build your house, Gloria.'

'We do need to speak to him,' the Queen said.

'We are beginning to be a little disappointed by promises made and their lack of fulfilment. We are happy to accept your offer to take us up there.'

Austin smiled and raised his can of Piton lager. The Queen had refused water from the plastic bottle and had taken a Coke: now he wondered if she had slipped a shot of rum into the glass. Who were the others who would accompany her tomorrow? Why did she speak in the plural, when she had clearly come out on her own? Not for the first time, he considered dumping his client altogether – but the takings at the bar hadn't been bad: the Canadians had been thirsty and the feminists had gone for passion fruit daiquiris in double digits. Maybe Mrs Smith would even lead him to the shiny green stones spotted by Jolene in the white handbag. And perhaps she did have an accomplice or a friend in the travel agency business who would bring luck and money to Austin Ford.

The Queen, in turn, began to realise that she must show her continuing gratitude to the man who, having given her shelter for one night, now seemed prepared to put her up tonight as well. She would not be exposed to the glare of publicity and global hysteria the disappearance of the monarch of Great Britain and her dependencies would be bound to occasion. He would help find the contractor who had failed to build No. 5 Bananaquit Drive. He might, even, know someone who knew what had happened to the necklace the Queen had so carefully packed away in her bag. Obviously, he wanted to talk about his family – especially his Auntie May. So he must; and she was prepared to listen.

But somehow it didn't turn out like that. The Queen could not say whether her deliciously sweet concoction from the bar (Boofy's girl had left half a fruit punch and the Queen had been brought up to hate waste), plus the Coke one of the American women had abandoned on a table accounted for the manner in which she now found herself addressing her new friend. Even she could tell her voice was stilted and high, unsuitable for a private conversation, but, as Austin answered her polite questions – How old is Auntie May? Does she get out much? Does she have far to go if she visits a shop? – she also knew that a transformation had taken place and she could no longer hide her secret from him. Just like the confessing recipient of a royal visit, she knew she would be guilty of the crime of holding back if she did not speak.

It had been a long two days. The plane, the irritation of the Bostocks and the knowledge they must have recognised her earlier by the TV, the unaccustomed standing and bending as she dutifully served beer, rum and cocktails to the tourists, not to mention the disappointment at finding a comfortable villa did not await her on arrival at St Lucia – all these were probable contributors to a new, almost reckless mood.

Austin had now gone through the lives of his first and second wives and was moving on to his second family in Trinidad and his uncle in Martinique when the unpredictable Mrs Smith leaned forward, sipped her drink and said in a high voice that there was something she must tell Ford and that it concerned Windsor Castle in the War.

'De war?' Austin cracked open his Piton lager and stared at the old lady. 'What you goin' on about?' he added, tipping the bottle down his throat. 'Windsor Village here, not Castle, Gloria.'

But the memory had to be told. The Queen would never know whether the constant reminder of her name in the letters proclaiming Windsor Village had triggered the sudden total recall of a winter evening, a basement in the Castle, planes and bombers overhead. 'The King. His late Majesty King George the Sixth – he came to find me down there – we were in danger and he said he had to tell me – I was thirteen years old, he was so brave, you know – "In case anything happens to us, you need to hear there is a secret – a secret in our family, Lilibet..."'

'What all this?' Austin began. Then he stopped. The moon had risen higher and it now showed the furthest margin of the beach, the raffia-roofed huts and the ghostly form of white plastic loungers. There was nobody there – unless you could count a black circular object poking out from under the fringe of a grass hut further up the beach. But

Austin knew the sounds of the bay and the rain-forest, and what he now heard did not belong to them. He held up his hand; and Mrs Smith fell silent.

The Beach

The sea lapped the shore, the moon shed an uneven light on the carefully raked beach, behind the band-stand the artificial lawns glowed green in the light of the security lamps. A kind of complicity reigned, between the bulky shadow of the Gros Piton and the two figures on their loungers, as if the stories being told were somehow guarded by the ancient, massive rock: already a part of history, the tales and reminiscences which now poured from Mrs Gloria Smith took shape against the deep darkness of the water at the Piton's base.

'You must have wondered, Ford, why one left the United Kingdom and came here?' demanded the Queen. 'What was the plan, what constituted so momentous a decision?'

Austin made no reply and his companion went on, as the moon appeared to grow nearer and the hair of the old lady with secrets shone on her head like a crown of white feathers. 'One has the duty, would you not agree, Ford, to set out the tapestry of one's life, to supply for the future a true account of one's encounters and decisions... In short, Ford, one is here to write. Yes, the autobiography of the Queen!'

Austin pulled a long-forgotten bag of toffees from his trouser pocket and popped two into his mouth, allowing the mulch of caramel and beer to swirl and form a coating on his teeth. He had an unpleasant feeling that someone was watching – or listening – and what would people think of Austin Ford if they saw him with this batty old woman on the beach? He sucked harder, causing his mumble of a reply to be indistinct; and Mrs Smith, clearly believing she heard encouragement for her new-found vocation, went piercingly on. 'To return to Windsor Castle – where one will open the volume one was told very firmly, very firmly indeed, not to tell anyone. In case the King and Queen were... The bombing was at its most ferocious at that time and in the event of Windsor being strafed – if that was the word – and one happened to be the sole survivor...'

'Yeah, that's for sure,' Austin said. He was aware of not having listened to the confidences granted him by Mrs Gloria Smith – but truly, she was worse than Auntie May, who at least only thought she had been on exotic journeys to the Pole or some such place. This Gloria appeared to be basing her fantasies here: and the likelihood of Windsor Village, so Austin thought, of suffering a bombing attack was nil. They wouldn't come up from Cuba, their planes were too old, like their beaten-up old cars, and he couldn't see Hewanorra Airport granting a Cuban pilot a landing, even if they came pretending to be tourists. Anyway, why would they go for his Rum Shop and a small assortment of half-built houses, Caribbean gingerbread houses that weren't even worth blowing up? No, Gloria was a bore; and he especially disliked the way her voice changed and her eyes went bright when she talked about this imaginary airborne invasion. It was time, before the full moon gave over to a pale sun waiting its turn to rise in the sky, to organise the departure of a disappointing client, remove her from the books of the Escort Service forever, and tell that ancient English couple up at the Joli Hotel to take care of their compatriot and help her on her way home.

'Ford!'

Now the woman was speaking in a tone which suggested she was about to issue an order. 'Who the hell do you think you are?' Austin muttered under his breath, before saying, 'Yes, Mrs Smith?' like a well-trained escort replying to a wealthy old lady. For God's sake, it should be he who was bossing *her* about. She'd spent two nights in the Rum Shop: what was it she expected of him now?

'Of course, it was Uncle David who took the

emeralds. Daddy knew that; one never really knew whether Mummy did. He was made to hand them back: it all comes to one, you know, Ford, if one thinks hard enough about that dreadful time when England was in such danger...'

'Musta been a pain,' Austin agreed lazily, but now with a touch of slyness in his voice. 'The emeralds, eh?' he added, as if he didn't care about the answer. 'Your old man give 'em to you when you was a girl? And so where are they now, I wonder?'

'Who knows?' Austin Ford's client replied crossly. 'They were taken from the handbag' – and with a sharp look over her shoulder as if to pick out the criminal from an identity parade, Mrs Smith gazed across the beach and back to the deserted tennis court where a couple of fallen coconuts sat in a pool of water caused by the sporadic showers from the rainforest. 'Lettice would never have left it unattended... too careless for words.'

Austin Ford tried to conceal his sudden interest in what his client was saying, by stretching out on the plastic lounger and closing his eyes. Maybe – just maybe – this Gloria Smith had seen someone, while she lay resting at the Joli Hotel, someone who came in and stole her money, her passport and the emeralds. If her memory was as great as she claimed, the details might come back to her. Then Austin could go and get them off the robber. But, as he well knew, the trouble with white people was that they thought all black people looked alike. If only she knew that black people considered whites to be identical, interchangeable – but there was no point in trying to explain this to Mrs Smith. The thought wouldn't have crossed her mind.

'It was always Uncle David. You wouldn't have been born then, Ford – but do you know, I wonder, who one is talking about? His Royal Highness – his wife, Wallis Simpson, not allowed to be a Royal Highness, which he did mind terribly, but what could we do? It was known – as an appalling secret, of course, and just to a handful of people – that Uncle David was on the side of Hitler in the war. He was so jealous of the King, my poor father...'

'Nothin' you could do,' Austin said in a sympathetic tone. He'd give it a go just a bit longer, then he'd get her up to reception and find those two dinosaurs and just dump her on them. A few minutes more of this and he'd go cuckoo anyway – unless, all at once, she could solve the mystery of the missing necklace.

'Daddy said that Uncle David had married – a French girl – when he was frightfully young. She'd had a child. A son. Yes, a son.'

Austin now yawned openly. The subject of the emeralds had vanished, just like the stones: maybe they were jinxed, like one time his employer Mr King had warned him when he took the ring from his little velvet bag out of the cupboard and insisted on Ford polishing the diamond surround. 'They're bad luck, Ford, especially this one from the Maharajah of Jaipur...'

'The French... mother... died, so one heard after the War,' Mrs Smith was saying. 'But her son – her son should have been crowned King. His existence was the secret confided by His Majesty King George the Sixth to his elder daughter, Princess Elizabeth, who is before you now, and speaking as your Queen.'

This was enough. Austin rose to his feet and made a purposeful gesture, a sign he was leaving the Joli Beach and the Rum Shop together, and indicating to Mrs Smith that she was expected to accompany him asap. But the old biddy didn't budge. What would he have to do to get her out of his hair for once and for all? Anyone could see she was crazy; and Austin blamed himself for having listened to her crap memories in the first place.

By now, however, there was no stopping the flow; and, like a spectator who must stand and watch the drama, Austin found himself rooted to the moonlit beach, unable to escape the stories and assertions, the occasional guarded tone which represented remorse or regret, the dry-ice enunciation of a woman who must always be obeyed. There had been a sister, he understood that – a sister whose heart had been broken and who had then gone on to have a son by a man then banished from the kingdom; there had been the folly of a woman, Diana, who had an inherited madness; there was a son who had married but his marriage was not valid.

Austin lifted one leg and then another; they felt like boulders of stone. Something in the old lady had him enchanted and petrified. He couldn't move, even into the softly lapping sea.

Then what appeared at first to be help could be seen coming down the beach from the Rainforest Bar. Framed by the vast bulk of the Gros Piton, marching with resolve over the crushed coral sand, three dark-suited men and one stout, fast-walking woman also in black, bore down on the loungers and Tahitian grass huts where Austin Ford sat with the Queen.

'Oh-oh,' Austin let out, as he saw his companion frown apprehensively at the approach of the strangers. 'What they want here, I'm sayin'...'

But before he could say any more, Austin Ford found himself gripped firmly by his client Gloria and whisked into the Rum Shop. The sill was pulled up and then, with surprising strength for a woman of her age, Mrs Gloria Smith pulled shut and locked the door.

The Search

When the team sent to assess and bring back the Queen of England from St Lucia had toured the small compound and found no trace of her – or of a Mr Ford they had been told about by a near-hysterical Lady Bostock at the Joli Hotel – they turned and went back along the beach. A phone line had been set up to enable confidential calls from Prince Charles in the manager's room at the Rainforest Bar – and although this had been hacked into and details of the search for the Queen globally transmitted, a decision had been taken to the effect that mobile phones were even less to be trusted (as previous experience with the heir to the throne and his widely overheard reference to Tampax had demonstrated) than the line just installed. Thus it was that billions heard a distinctly testy Prince of Wales inform his team that they must find Her Majesty and that a psychiatric report on the state of her mental health must be emailed to him directly at Highgrove. If necessary, the patient should be sedated before boarding a plane home. Disruption might follow an attempt to restrain the Queen; and for all those who had enjoyed the play and film by Alan Bennett, a vision of *The Madness of King George* rose before the eyes. Was it possible that the sensible, well-balanced woman the world had known as the monarch of Great Britain – horse-loving sportswoman, wife and mother – had actually lost her sanity? Kettles boiled but stood unused as the conversation continued. People in their baths allowed the water to go cold as they listened in on Radio Nine to the pirated conversation.

If the woman and three Scotland Yard detectives who made up the team sent out to restore the heir's mother to her rightful home in England mused on the fact that the sectioning of the Queen was tantamount to removing her from the throne, not one spoke out. They couldn't find their gracious sovereign; and one or two of the men felt a shiver of fear at the notion of imprisonment in the Tower as a result. This was a time when the veil between history and the present day seemed perilously thin: if they *did* find her, did the Queen have the powers to incarcerate them? (She did indeed have the right to arrest criminals.) All in all, it was a relief when the phone malfunctioned; and, using their mobiles, the hunters laid plans to tour the island, concentrating on the capital, Castries, where there had by now been several sightings of the Queen. For the sake of efficiency, a speedboat was ordered, to take them up the coast. They would be picked up by the helipad at the far end of Joli Bay.

The Queen and Austin Ford left the Rum Shop when the protracted silence indicated that the team had gone some time before – and even the greckle, a noisy bird, felt free to hop about outside and let out shrill calls. How it was that the hunters had not suspected their prey to be in the shop it was impossible to say: perhaps the idea of the Queen of England in a low bar – or the fact of the psychiatrist announcing that rum was likely, due to its naval associations (the tragic death of Lord Mountbatten came to mind) to be her very least favourite – had led them to thump a few times on the ramshackle building and retrace their footsteps to the beach and the Rainforest Bar. In any case, it was with a sigh of relief that the Queen came out and stood a moment later blinking in the first rays of the rising sun. Then Austin led her to the pier, called the Rasta who was dozing in his boat, and assisted his elderly client to embark. The outboard engine spluttered and roared.

So it was that the Queen and Austin Ford disappeared into the bay of Ravissant Estate, just before Prince Charles's contingent of medical and MI6 personnel circled the bay in their speedboat and then proceeded to head off in the opposite direction.

The Thief

'You didn't, Marianne! I simply can't believe you took – you stole, all these jewels! We must go back at once. I am staggered at your having done this –'

'Go back?' Lady Bostock repeated. 'We can't do that, Martyn. What about our holiday?'

'The holiday's off!' came the shouted reply. 'Pack! Go on! Start packing!'

The Bostocks, in their cottage on the Joli Estate, sat under a rain cloud by the plunge pool, on their heads white hats already sodden from the rainforest's sharp showers. Lady Bostock's hair, grey and streaked across her forehead, gave her the look of a child's drawing of a grown-up: a schoolteacher perhaps, or a representation of a doll left out in the wet. That tears now coursed down her cheeks failed to move Sir Martyn, who was blundering towards the veranda door leading into the cottage. He cursed as he almost slipped in a new puddle, and for a moment the bag he carried – 'not plastic', as Lady Bostock had been proud to announce in the restaurant the night before, 'a brown paper bag like the old days' – almost fell from his grasp into the blue chlorinated water of the pool. Both Bostocks screamed simultaneously. Then came a silence, even Sir Martyn appearing to resign himself to a state of uncertainty. A further drenching took place before the couple moved indoors: both knew the occupants of the slightly grander villa a few yards up the hill must be listening to Sir Martyn's accusations and his wife's increasingly feeble defence.

'The... the handbag was open on the bed,' Marianne Bostock now said. 'The – the green necklace was almost falling out of it...'

'I can't believe it,' was Sir Martyn's often-stressed comment. 'Give it all to me, for God's sake! You actually took this into dinner last night – Marianne, have you gone out of your mind?'

Lady Bostock said she had hoped one of the women dining in the Rainforest Bar would recognise the brown paper bag and claim the contents. 'I was waiting for someone to come forward, darling.' Placatory tone clearly not working, Lady Bostock summoned the energy to glare at her husband in a manner which reminded him of his lowly origins, in comparison at least with those of his in-laws, the seventeenth Earl of St Leger (who had had no need, in order to feel superior, to find himself knighted by the Queen).

'Don't shout,' Marianne reiterated, the second of these commands apparently successful, as Sir Martyn, sitting in the Harrods basket chair bought for the Joli Hotel by a disgraced estate agent specialising in bargains and repossessions and shipped by banana boat from Southampton, now slumped back, eyes closed, as if to show the extent of the disbelief already several times professed.

'You see,' Lady Bostock pressed her point, 'I was just passing the room and there was the white handbag on the bed and when I looked inside there were the – well they must be emeralds, Martyn, I ought to know when I see gems of that calibre.'

'And nothing else?' asked Sir Martyn, his own tone now defensive and suspicious. 'No money, no passport.' Again he assured his wife he found this hard to believe.

'Who leaves their door open, Martyn, and goes out?'

At this, there was another silence.

'Well, there may have been a few dollars,' came the next response. 'And yes. There was a passport. I handed it in to the concierge at reception. They looked up the owner, at my request, but there was no sign of her in the register. So I decided to wait, and restore the jewels myself. After all, you never can tell in these places who is working for the management and who is looking out for himself.'

'True,' Sir Martyn conceded. Both he and his wife refrained from mentioning the probable fate of

---

the dollars – and Sir Martyn had never been a man for noticing his wife's new silk top or sequinned pants, even if these had not been worn before on the holiday.

'She was – she was an elderly lady, but the passport photo didn't show her at all clearly,' Lady Bostock said. 'There was a photo slipped in, just a snap, I thought it rather sweet so I kept it.' She pulled at the brown paper bag, and after a swirl of stones with their diamond surrounds fell into her lap, she foraged for the picture.

'Oh my God!' cried both the Bostocks; and this time the gay couple in the grander villa up the hill came out on to the veranda and stood there like weathermen, keen to discover which way the wind was blowing. There had perhaps been a break-in at the cottage below, or a body had been found in the plunge pool – or, unlikely as it might seem in this day and age, the elderly Sir with the dog-faced wife might be homophobic. (But then, nothing about the Joli Estate seemed to belong to this day and age, being marooned in the fifties or even the thirties. You never can tell.)

The photograph purloined by Lady Bostock from the unattended handbag showed a green sward, marked with small towels, and a pair of green wellies at the end of the row. Bounding into the frame was a small dog, the speed of its movement blurring its brown head and distinctive white markings.

'This is what we have to do,' barked Sir Martyn, who had been known for his ruthless business methods and could asset strip as fast as any non-tax-paying City mogul.

'What can we do?' wailed Lady Bostock. The couple on the veranda above exchanged embarrassed glances: were the occupants of the cottage celebrating – and finding difficulty therein – a second honeymoon? They retired into the safety of their self-contained suite.

Sir Martyn placed the green stones back in the paper bag and had packed before his wife had even opened her suitcase. 'Come now!' thundered Sir Martyn Bostock, and for the first time in forty years of marriage, Marianne had no choice other than to obey.

'The airport,' her husband's stentorian tones rang out in the rained-over area just outside reception, where today only one run-down taxi awaited a fare. 'Fifty dollars if you speed up,' puffed Sir Martyn, dragging his wife in after him. And when the driver said in a slow drawl that fifty dollars was the price anyway, Marianne was able to witness for the first time in her life the acquiescence of a once-great businessman to an obviously bad deal.

As the Bostocks and the emeralds in the brown paper bag jolted their way to Vieux Fort and Hewanorra Airport, Sir Martyn rehearsed his wife on her approach to officials and customs brokers there. Lady Bostock had not found the necklace in her luggage when she arrived three days ago from London Gatwick on a Virgin Atlantic flight. It had gone into an inner flap of her case and she had only noticed it today. There was no connection between the discovery of the jewels and her husband's decision to end their holiday so abruptly and fly home today. An illness in the family was the cause. She and Sir Martyn would show their gratitude in every way they could if the contents of the brown paper bag could be handed in to Customs and they could leave on tonight's scheduled flight...

And so, as the Bostocks climbed out of the black car (which had been driven at exactly the same speed as any other journey to the airport) – and after Sir Martyn had paid the agreed hundred dollars, they pushed their way in through the crowd awaiting check-in at the airport, to find they must wait their turn before a suitable official could be entrusted with the emeralds.

As they stood in line, paper bag clutched to Lady Bostock's bosom, a small boat with a half-conked-out engine came ear-splittingly into Vieux Fort harbour and tied up at the wharf.

A slight, small woman wearing a lavender tweed skirt, flip-flops, a T-shirt with a picture of Gros Piton across the front and 'Love from St Lucia' printed below, stepped out of the boat on to the quay.

A battered-looking jeep drew up and the oddly-attired lady's escort, a man in his thirties, waved to the driver; then, without needing to give details of their destination, the couple were driven to Hewanorra Airport.

Arrival of the Incoming Flight

The Queen may have suffered criticism – of her role as a mother, of her voice and of the extent of her fortune – but no one could say of her that she lacked pragmatism and an ability to adapt to new circumstances as they presented themselves to her.

It had been obvious, especially after the agonising discomfort of a second night at the back of the Rum Shop, that the plan to live in a modest villa by the edge of the sea in a Commonwealth country had got off to a bad start. Her house was a hole in the ground; she had been robbed and left destitute; and hearing French spoken on the beach had reminded her of her dread of the new President of France, with his own form of pragmatism, this including, in his role as President also of the EU, the intro-duction of new laws unfriendly to the monarchy. It would be a relief to return to the country where, despite her German ancestry, the Queen was seen as the epitome of Englishness. Once home she could shore up the weakening realm, and rally the people who believed her to be a fixture that would last forever. She would be in Britain in time for the Opening of Parliament – and, for the first time since leaving the country, she thought of the Duke, walking beside her through the Lords assembled in their scarlet and gold robes. The Duke's finger, as so often on state occasions, would lie lightly on his sovereign's white-gloved hand. The thought was oddly comforting.

The Rasta's rickety boat with its ear-splitting engine had charged along the southern coastline of St Lucia for two hours before the conurbation that was Vieux Fort, its harbour and wharf, came into view. Austin Ford, who sat in the prow and gazed sulkily out to sea, was as deep in thought as his soon-to-be erstwhile client, Mrs Gloria Smith. It had been annoying that his employer Mr King, who Austin imagined would offer tea to the English lady and her escort, had said the meeting could not take place: Austin had set himself the task of finding the stolen Cambridge emeralds and had worked out how much he would ask Mr King to pay (in US dollars). His determination had been to demand a payment in advance from the King, who was the perfect buyer, obsessed with emeralds and, as far as Austin was concerned, a man of fabulous wealth. The payment would cover Mrs Gloria's fare back to the UK, for, as Austin knew from Jolene, her money and passport had also been stolen from the hotel bedroom. He was desperate, now, to get the owner of the jewels off the island. Jolene had a good idea of who'd done it: Rover from Soufrière, who'd already been arrested several times for petty theft. It was just a question of getting this strange woman off his back – and taking a few pals to have a word with Rover. As it was, he'd had to dig deep into his savings to find enough for an economy seat to London. A new passport was easy – Campbell at the airport had been alerted by Austin and had ready a leather (imitation) purple passport with *Dieu et mon Droit* stamped under the lion and the unicorn and a photo of an old lady (a copy found on the floor of the booth of the Polaroid shot of a traveller). There would be no suspicions at the replication: old women, after all, and especially if they were white, all looked exactly alike.

Austin sighed as the engine cut out and the red-painted fishing boat drew up to the wharf. He had been surprised at the equanimity of Mrs Smith at the realisation she was being taken to Hewanorra Airport, by sea, and not on a touristic jaunt to the coves and cocoa plantations of the south of the island. She was a tad gone in the head, of course, but really she was behaving like this was a royal visit and the duration of it just what she had been told beforehand. Look at her now! The woman was standing in the boat waiting to be helped out on to the quay and as a bunch of children ran past and waved to her, she was graciously waving back at them. She'd been rich and important once, that was obvious if you knew about the emeralds; or maybe she'd been married to a man like Sir Richard Branson, who might build a new resort in the hills above Soufrière and pay better money to Jolene, Jooleeta and Austin's other cousins and girlfriends than the Joli Hotel. Austin even wondered if he could ask Mrs Smith if she *was* Lady Branson in disguise.

Such musings were interrupted by the arrival of the incoming flight from London Gatwick, a jumbo with a Marilyn-imitation blonde painted on its prow and HOTLIPS written in large letters under a perky breast. The Queen stood obediently in line as passengers emerged from the transatlantic aircraft; and as they descended to the reception area and baggage hall she looked modestly down, as if avoiding both recognition and the possible necessity of recognising someone or something herself. The sight of her feet, beach-stained and streaked with dirt from the tarmac on Joli Estate roads caused her to look up again quickly – and it was then that the double shock occurred. For a passenger bearing the News section of the *Sunday Times* was now visible behind the plate glass dividing about-to-be travellers and new arrivals; and the headline QUEEN IN CARIBBEAN appeared, at least to the Queen, to dwarf almost everything else in the airport and to draw the eyes of the crowd, much as she had on her royal tours, always done. That she was known to be in St Lucia was of little interest to her – for, like the holidays organised for the poor, one place was made to look just like another (a camp, a pool, a bar and an eatery for Her Majesty's low-paid subjects, a red carpet, a ritual ceremony by painted people and a motorcade for the Queen).

No, it was the unpleasant experience of seeing oneself after three days without so much as a royal event recorded, three days without the continual intrusion of the hungry lens, which had made the Queen unaccustomed to representations of herself, Queen and Head of State, symbol of Britain's enduring monarchy and the proud island's refusal to throw off the pomp and glory. For the woman occupying the entire front page of the newspaper seemed to bear no relation to the general perception of Elizabeth the Second. The white hair floated in all directions, a T-shirt with an image of Gros Piton with a naked woman dancing wildly below (there had been no choice: suffering from the afternoon heat while serving customers at the Rum Shop, she had pillaged Austin's meagre cupboard within) hung limply over the Queen's bust. The shot went mercilessly on down to the flip-flops, passing a terminally rumpled tweed skirt and ending with a puddle of rum on the floor of the half-finished village, this visited by a mangy-looking black cat. Who could have taken this terrible photograph? And as the indignant thought crossed her

193

mind, the Queen also realised she knew the answer: the American tourist of course, the man who hadn't been a part of the group visiting Austin's establishment for a shot of authenticity. He had suddenly understood who she was... and she remembered her dislike of the camera as it edged up close to her and the man smiled as it came ever closer...

The next shock was almost expected, for, just like the first time the Queen had had to put up with the rudeness of the Bostocks, the glares and stares commenced as soon as they turned to examine the amount of people behind them and were granted a sight of the Queen identical to that in the Sunday paper still clearly visible through the plate glass. No one could have believed their monarch could transform herself into the debauched, confused-looking woman in the shot – and where was the Duke? Had she been the victim of a fun outing organised by the well-meaning Fergie? But everyone, once they made the connection – its effects were now clearly visible on the faces of the Bostocks and an aristocratic-looking woman at the head of the queue had begun to stare at the Queen as if an UFO or some other unaccountable denizen of a mythical world were amongst those going Virgin Atlantic to the UK – everyone would find those perceptions ineradicably altered by this new appearance of the Queen.

As Austin Ford sighed, lit another Marlboro

Light and stamped his feet on the ground in time with his iPod selection, the Bostocks made their assault.

'It is,' Lady Bostock said shrilly. 'Of course it is, Martyn!'

'It can't be.'

'It *is*. Keep my place in the queue. I'm going – going down to – to ...'

'Watch out,' Sir Martyn boomed. 'What if she's not the Queen? For God's sake, it's very unlikely. Stay here, Marianne!'

'I'm going,' Lady Bostock announced in a whisper that came out with the force of a shriek.

And this was how, rebutting Austin as he attempted to stand between his client Mrs Smith and the mad woman from the Joli Hotel, Lady Bostock treated the travellers at Hewanorra Airport to a display of home-grown ritual never seen before in St Lucia and remembered even in England only by those presented at Court half a century ago.

Lady Bostock was far taller than the Queen (especially in the beach shoes which gave no extra height) but it was with a certain grace that she sank into a curtsey and remained, bent low with head almost touching the floor of the airport hall, for several minutes.

'What she do, Gloria?' Austin asked his client.

Then, everything seemed to happen at once. The passenger holding the *Sunday Times* collected her baggage and came back into the hall to find a friend

– and, as Austin saw the image of Mrs Smith on the front page of the paper she carried, he let out a cry and stamped his feet harder to the beat from his iPod. As Lady Bostock rose, wobbling a little by now, from the deep obeisance to her monarch, the brown paper bag containing the emeralds burst from inside her blouse and scattered over the floor.

The Queen and Lady Bostock stood and stared at the jewels as they coiled amongst the cigarette stubs, discarded hot dogs and other rubbish in the hall.

Austin Ford later complained to his friend Rover at the Sunset Bar in Soufrière that he'd had a hard time, caught between those two women – but he was happy, if this was what they wanted, that his client had accepted the necklace from the crazy lady – and, when a cache of US dollars had also been found to be lurking in the brown paper bag, she had repaid Austin for her ticket (Economy it must remain: the Queen hated extravagance) and had added an extremely modest tip for his services over the past days.

'I say God save the Queen,' Austin said piously to his friend.

The Return

As the huge Boeing thundered down the runway, the Queen sat forward in her seat (she was in the central block in Economy and it was virtually impossible to see out of a window) and peered at the rain drips accumulating on the aircraft's wing. They reminded her of Balmoral, her threatened castle and estate, where rambling over cleuch and moor would no longer be her prerogative: where the rain, coming down democratically from heaven, would pour on commoners and princes alike.

It was a shame; but she was glad to be on her way home. She was needed there – and even if Charles had acted too precipitately by sending a team out to look for her on the island, it was proof that the sovereign's powers still held: without Her Majesty Queen Elizabeth the Second Parliament could not open, and the country would fall into uncertainty and, worse, anarchy. Some upstart

EMMA TENNANT

would come along and claim the throne; and the Queen shuddered as she imagined Princess Michael of Kent in the Crown Jewels and reading from a speech prepared by some interior decorator chosen for his designs of a new Buckingham Palace.

No! It was unthinkable. If the Queen wondered why she had left in the first place, the thought did not haunt her for long: there were certain things one did and no one expected one to feel remorseful. There just wasn't time in the packed schedule of a reigning monarch to look back with guilt or speculation at how things could have turned out. For the Queen there could never be a 'road not taken': there was no alternative to being the Queen.

The same went for people, what the newspapers called relationships. They could only be measured against the powers of the Head of State, and because of this must always take second place to familial or conjugal ties (the dogs, who did not know the position of their mistress at the pinnacle of the country's aristocracy and greater in stature than Archbishop or Prime Minister, were exempted from this hierarchical arrangement, and because of this the Queen loved them more than all her subjects).

A stewardess was doing the rounds with a drinks trolley and the Queen suffered the discomfort of an enormous paunched man leaning right across her to trumpet his multiple order of lager. His wife followed suit by ordering gin and tonic (the Queen invariably assumed the matrimonial state to prevail when confronted by adult strangers: it was easier that way to get through an arduous royal tour, which would have undergone delays if 'partners' – the Queen was not yet quite sure what these could be – or people who had separated, had to be distinguished from the rest. After all, it wasn't so long ago that divorcees had been refused admission to the garden parties and balls at the Palace).

'And two Pringles,' the woman went on. Two tins were handed to her and a thin biscuit-like object slid out, followed by a good many more. The tonic water teetered dangerously on the edge of the woman's tray as a slight turbulence teased the plane, and one of the miniature bottles of gin fell to the floor, letting out a strong smell.

'You OK love?' the fat man's wife said to the Queen as a wetness crept into the uncomfortable rubber flip-flops and the Queen shifted away from her neighbours. 'Sorry about that!' But, as the Queen knew and this woman would never be able to understand, these people were infinitely preferable to the Bostocks, the latter safely ensconced in Upper Class.

By the time the plane had risen above the mountainous, forested shores of St Lucia and the seatbelt sign was off, the Queen decided she would make for the toilets at the back of Economy and try to wash the all-pervasive smell of gin from her feet. It brought memories of rainy days at Sandringham

and gin-and-tonics partaken of by Lady Lettice
Farquhar in the kitchen of their farmhouse, while
the dogs rushed in and out, shaking wet coats on to
the Queen's tweed skirt. It made her sad – but she
couldn't say why – she was going back, was she
not? Lady Lettice would be expected to be in waiting and they would exchange little anecdotes about
the corgis and the weather as they always did. (Mrs
McDuff would have looked after the dogs, of
course, while Her Majesty was 'on leave', an expression which came to the Queen as she edged her
way up the aisle: she had been on leave like a
member of her own armed forces, and now she was
returning to her country to do her duty.) It did not
occur to her that her son Charles might have
organised another team, to interrogate the monarch
and examine the extent of her insanity: he had
accepted by now, surely, that his mother would for
a long time yet hold the reins. Why, the people
he'd sent hadn't even been able to find her! Charles
would be an old man before he came to the throne.

The Queen, unable to pass a trolley from which
the stewardess extricated plastic trays and proceeded to distribute them to the couples and children in the packed plane, had never before found
her passage blocked; there had never been an
impediment on the well-planned circulatory tours
of the Palace gardens to the sovereign's progress
over well-mown lawns; doors opened magically on
every tour of inspection. She coughed delicately –

as Lady Lettice might have done, to announce her presence to royalty – but no one budged, indeed she had to step backwards as the trolley grazed her stomach in its onward crawl down the plane.

'Are you in need of the toilet, madam?' An officious-looking man (lower middle-class, the Queen thought, but it was so hard nowadays to place people) had risen from his aisle seat and was waving to the stewardess, whose apparent inability to see the Queen had contributed to her first-and-only experience of what it was like to be invisible. 'Can you let this lady pass?' the officious man added, and he now came out to stand in the aisle himself, just above the trolley, as if to arrest all movement until his command was obeyed.

The Queen found herself permitted a small slice of space between the meal wagon and the blocks of economy seats, and with an appreciative murmur (again, how did one address someone in these circumstance? Where are you from, as had been learned with the Bostocks, was inappropriate; and anyway, he looked like a man who would reply with something like 'Row Fourteen Seat Six' to a royal query or show of interest). Definitely, she must push on: the occupants of the row behind had now noticed the smell of alcohol and were looking suspiciously at the frail-looking woman with dishevelled white hair, a loud T-shirt and (once these came into view several passengers shrugged or giggled) the offending gin-soaked flip-flops. The toilets, still seemingly miles away at the rear of the aircraft, must be reached as soon as possible and order restored.

A queue had formed outside both port and starboard toilets by the time the Queen reached the end of the aisle. People – mainly women – went in and an extraordinary length of time passed before they emerged made-up, cologne-scented or whatever. Clearly they had not given a thought for the convenience of others; and the Queen was mildly shocked, having adhered during all the long (and frequently exhausting) half-century and more of her reign to the belief that oneself must always come last. That she was not enjoying this example of her oft-repeated dictum was an unfortunate truth; but, like the queues in blitzed London which the Queen Mother had on occasion visited, these recorded by Pathe News, she saw they were just something that had to be put up with. So it was as a housewife in the War that the Queen consoled herself for her long wait.

Edging forward, it was possible to see a young man, slickly dressed in Paul Smith and sporting handmade leather shoes, who sat hunched over his laptop in the penultimate row of Economy. The seat beside him was empty, a mohair coat, ready for the exigencies of British weather, thrown across it – and the impression was given of privileges conferred, of this man's being a part of a new wealthy class the Queen would not know or recognise.

Despite her eyes being now fixed on his screen, the young banker – or hedge-fund manager or financial adviser, did not look up or choose to exchange any kind of human signal with the old lady who now peered at the Channel Four news showing on the young man's mobile phone, this strapped to his wrist

The laptop and the phone both carried the same message, but the Queen, accustomed to the voice and manner of the presenter Jon Snow, chose Channel Four news as the medium now informing her – and the rest of the world – that a story had just broken of a true heir to the throne for the British Isles and of a 'triumph' for the genealogist who had worked so long on uncovering him. This 'heir', by profession a traffic warden, had been found, so the news presenter Jon Snow announced, after years of painstaking research and – slipped in as if of little importance by the presenter – the conclusive proof of a DNA test. The news had only just come from the genealogist's home in the Channel Islands.

Then came shots of people – most of them irritatingly foreign tourists when the TV station desperately needed the reaction of true Brits – giving their opinion on this astounding discovery. Some were bored, others had no idea, apart from the existence of the Queen, of anyone being expected to inherit the crown. An old lady, probably a contemporary of the monarch, started on a long and passionate speech on the subject of the British Constitution and the need for there to be a written constitution – but the cameras dodged away before the words European Union could be mentioned and a blonde girl, Swedish and only in her first week on an English language course, was found by the railings at Buckingham Palace, giving 'I very like William' as her response to all questions.

'Sorry, can I get past?' A bad-tempered-looking woman in her forties shoved the Queen rudely in the ribs; and it was only then that it became clear to her that the queue was at last stretching behind her and not ahead. A friend of the bad-tempered woman now queue-jumped to the head of the line, laughing as she went past, 'A pretender? It's like the history books!' And the door of the WC was wrenched open before anyone could complain. 'Time for a republic is what I say,' came with another roar of laughter. 'Kings, Queens – who cares?' And with that and a deafening flush from the lavatory behind the still-open door, the subject of inheritance was dismissed.

The Ride Home

The Queen sat upright in a superannuated minicab as it wove its way through dense traffic on the M25 from Gatwick to London. No one in any of the cars bad-temperedly driven by men late for meetings or women determined on a shopping trip in the city, recognised the slight, white-haired figure – though one group of children perched in the back of a people carrier laughed and pointed at the old lady in the T-shirt with bright, tropical colours. Rain was falling and the skies made a lid which appeared to seal off the landscape, so it lay like a grey blanket in all directions. It was warm, even hot; and the contrast with the rainforest conditions recently enjoyed by Mr Santander's passenger was not great: here, as in St Lucia, the weather conditions brought a longing for Balmoral, the cool of the hills there and a rain sweeter than the metallic drops falling on the motorway.

The fact of being in a minicab (another unknown experience for the Queen) brought her recent arrival on the Caribbean island to mind, and Alvyne with his plastic Christmas tree appeared before the Queen's eyes, alongside her present driver's postcard of palms and blue sea pinned just above the dashboard. Did people always dream of being where they were not, the Queen wondered; if in a cold climate did they yearn for the equator, if in a banana plantation did they pine for snow? It seemed that no one could live without the secret hope of an opposite to what they had been dealt in life.

And now she, the Queen of England, had become for the first time identical to her subjects. She had wanted something else; she had wanted things to be different. Of course, those people to whom she spoke on walkabouts and tours did not bring up the subject of their disappointing holidays or of failed attempts at settling in the country they had chosen to emigrate to: it would have looked as if another attempt had been the real cause of their going away, that of escaping the country over which she reigned. All the same, the Queen sensed the need of apparently docile and placid Britons to travel, see the world and maybe not return; and again, the memory of the suitcase on the top of the wardrobe in the East End and the ill-received queries by the Duke on seeing it there, came back to her. People wanted to feel they could take off, get out, be free of worrying responsibilities – just as she had. That she now understood them better brought a feeling of resolution to the Queen. There *were* other places than Britain; but she had made a choice to pick up where she left off, as if Brno had never existed with his passports and travel tickets; as if she hadn't succumbed to the notion of buying off-plan and had never really had any desire to see her new life take shape out there. A monarch cannot indulge in regrets: too many resonances of heads cut off and kings and queens exiled overseas all their lives for a lack of decisive reigning presented themselves. The Queen had been gone three days; and, like the son of God, would be perceived as having risen from the dead. If, as she pondered, her absence had meant anything at all – but, there was no denying the fact, it would have meant a great deal, not mentioning the chaos liable to succeed the disappearance of a Head of State. And what lay on the verges of the road they travelled along would provide the proof.

For the thoughts and reminiscences of the Queen had taken up the drive, and despite Mr Santander's sudden cheeky interpolation: 'You like a new king, madam?' as a radio station muttered away and people were brought in to give their opinions on the need for a monarchy, this had been a restful journey, less ringed round with anxious lackeys than the gold coach on its way to the Houses of Parliament, and just as important to the history

EMMA TENNANT

books – the townscape the Queen knew so well had come into view.

Flowers, just as she had glimpsed on TV in the reception of the Joli Hotel, made a cellophane sea in St James's and in Hyde Park. In the Mall, balloons floated above the heads of a huge crowd, making progress impossible, and Mr Santander sat back, eyes closed, while speaking softly and at length in Spanish on his mobile phone. 'Where you want to go, lady?' came now in English – for his passenger had specified only Buckingham Palace and he sincerely wished he had not taken her instruction, thus losing further fares. They'd be here all day, at this rate.

'This will do,' said his passenger as they nudged up to the gates of the Palace. 'One will get out here.'

Mr Santander noticed that the Palace railings, with their array of soft toys, bouquets and lipstick-written expressions of love for the vanished Queen of England were paraded by police – and for the first time since picking up this innocuous old lady, he felt alarmed. Why did she want to come here? Would she cry like people after the death of Princess Diana? Was there a book of condolence here to be signed, in memory of the Queen?

Then, looking in the driving mirror, he saw his fare closely, as she leaned forward to open the door of the minicab. Simultaneously, the live radio show went into overdrive: the Queen had been spotted, in a car at Putney, then crossing Hammersmith Bridge – here was the number-plate – could it be? – could it be true that she had come back? The woman announcer's voice came thick with indecision and the lack of real news.

Before an answer could be heard, an enormous cheer went up in the Mall. It swept up and engulfed the Palace; the gates swung open; and five policemen cleared the way for Mr Santander's battered conveyance. There was no choice but to go, past saluting Horse Guards, to the entrance to the monarch's official London residence.

The Balcony

Hours later – there had been endless discussions with the Chamberlain, Prince Charles and at least five other bureaucrats – the flag over Buckingham Palace, at half mast in the absence of the Queen, went up and the roar from the waiting crowd swelled out and over St James's Park and down to Trafalgar Square. Those who demanded to see the Queen were rewarded, just as the autumn light was fading, with a spotlit balcony, the Duke and the Queen's children in full uniform, and finally the slight figure of the monarch herself as she stepped out to acknowledge the relief and adoration of the crowd.

The Queen was wearing, on this occasion of her return from a brief visit to a Commonwealth country, a well-pressed lavender tweed suit (two of everything was invariably ordered, for the royal wardrobe, and this did indeed now seem to have been a wise precaution, much appreciated at the time by the late Norman Hartnell). Round her neck – rather unusually for the monarch, who did not like to appear dressy in the daytime, was an emerald necklace and in her ears shone the same green stones, another part of the parure stolen in the Joli Hotel; the diamond surrounds winking down at the crowd in the bright lights.

After waving from the balcony for an unprecedentedly long time, the Queen turned to walk indoors. Lady Lettice would be waiting for her there – and, of course, the corgis.

A last swell of noise went up as the people saw her go. And a long, appreciative sound very like laughter, when the shiny white handbag, reassuringly empty, came into view. The English were a strange race, Mr Santander thought, as he backed the minicab nervously to the Palace gates.

THE END